OR
WAS HE
PUSHED?

OR
WAS HE
PUSHED?

Richard Lockridge

J. B. Lippincott Company
Philadelphia and New York

I am in debt to John Gallaway for information, from an
expert in the field, on the functioning of advertising agencies.
He is not, of course, responsible for any mistakes I may
have made. They are entirely my own.

R.L.

U.S. Library of Congress Cataloging in Publication Data

Lockridge, Richard, birth date
  Or was he pushed?

  I. Title.
PZ3.L811440r   [PS3523.0245]   813'.5'2   75–2007
ISBN–0–397–01080–X

For Hildy

OR
WAS HE
PUSHED?

1

SHE SAID SOMETHING in a drowsy voice, but she was turned away from him in the wide bed and he could not make out what she had said. It was possible, of course, that she was murmuring in her sleep. Drowsiness can be an aftermath. Tony Cook said, "Hmm?" softly so as not to waken her—not yet to waken her.

"Since I was much younger," Rachel said. This time the words were a little clearer. "I've told you that." Then she turned to lie on her back beside him. "Almost since I was a little girl. The thing is, you just don't listen."

"Yes, dear," Tony said. "Told me what?"

"About wanting to be an actress," Rachel Farmer said. "Only I'm too tall. I'd have to play opposite a basketball player. Only Mr. Bradley says it calls for a tall girl. And photogenic. And he thinks I'll be able to read all right. He says the test came out O.K. He says a little more Brooklyn, if I can manage it, because

9

Gloria's supposed to come from Brooklyn. Anyway, she doesn't seem to say much before she's killed."

Tony raised himself on an elbow and looked down on her. It was a hot July night in Manhattan, in the second-floor apartment on Gay Street, and she was wearing nothing to impede the view.

"Photogenic you are," he told her. "Brooklyn I wouldn't have thought. And who the hell is Mr. Bradley? and Gloria, for that matter? Except that she gets killed. You've lost me, darling."

"Advertising," Rachel said. "I've posed for them quite a lot in the last couple of years. Photographs, mostly, but some sketches. Dresses, mostly. But now and then furs. A sable, one time. And it must have been a hundred and ten in the studio. I thought he'd never get the shot he wanted. And I was supposed to be climbing a flight of stairs."

Tony Cook remembered the photograph; she had shown it to him, reproduced in *The New Yorker*. She hadn't looked hot. She had looked lovely, and precisely like a woman who should be wearing sables. (Not, of course, that he had ever known one. Detectives, even if first grade, seldom encounter girls in sable coats.) Tony lowered his head to the pillow, but lay so that he could look at her. With some effort, he directed his mind to the subject at hand, whatever it might be.

"This man Bradley," he said. "He's going to make a movie. Is that it? And give you a part in it?" Abruptly, he sat up. "In *Hollywood*?" he said. There was apprehension in his voice.

She turned toward him, and her head moved negatively on the pillow. She had let her dark hair grow long again. It lay across her right shoulder and almost covered her right breast.

"No," Rachel said. "Right here in New York, Tony.

On location. It's for TV—a pilot is what they call it. Film. But they hope it will be a series. 'Brook No Evil,' Mr. Bradley says it's called."

Tony found his attention was wandering. But not far. With some difficulty, he recalled it. He said, "When?"

Rachel said, "When what?"

"This movie. The pilot. Pilot film? What you were talking about."

"When the script's approved, Mr. Bradley says. If Miss Claymore is free then. Peggy Claymore. We saw her last winter. In something called *After Hours*. The critics didn't think much of the play, but all three of them liked her. When she was onstage, you were sending out rays. Don't *do* that, Tony."

"Just sending out rays," Tony told her. "I—well, I didn't think you minded."

"You distract me. You don't care at all that maybe I'm going to get to be an actress."

"I am very happy for you, Miss Farmer," Tony said. He spoke formally, as if they both had clothes on. "I never send out rays toward five-feet two-inch blondes. Even when they have reddish hair."

"See," she said. "You do remember Peggy Claymore. She's the kind most men do, I guess. Anyway, she's going to play Enid Brook. That's why it's called 'Brook No Evil.' Paul and Enid Brook. They're private detectives. In the pilot, Mr. Bradley says, they find out who killed me. That is, Gloria. *Tony.*"

"Go on telling me about this movie—pilot—you're going to have a part in. It's very interesting, darling. This Peggy Claymore plays a private detective and you play—"

"You expect me to think what I'm saying when you're—"

"No," Tony said. "This is no time for a—"

"Then just quit talking—oh, oh."

"Yes," Tony said. "Oh, yes. *Yes.*"

They quit talking.

After they had shared a shower, Rachel sat in a summer robe and watched him while he dressed. "You've got one end longer than the other," she said about his necktie, and he retied it. Then he sat beside her on the sofa in the living room and poured them very small drinks from the cognac bottle. It had got to be a little after one of Sunday morning but, for once, Sunday was Tony's day off.

"It isn't," Tony said, "that I'm not interested in this acting job of yours. You know that, don't you?"

"All right, Tony. First things first."

"For both of us?"

"For both of us. Only tomorrow you'll listen, won't you?"

"When we both have clothes on," Tony said, and stood up.

"That will make it easier," Rachel said, and watched Detective (1st gr.) Anthony Cook buckle on his shoulder holster with the off-duty .25 in it. He leaned down to kiss her good night. This time they kissed lightly.

At the door, Tony said, "About ten all right?"

"Yes, darling."

"And you'll remember the door chain?"

"Yes, Tony. I always remember the door chain."

It is not too many blocks from Gay Street—which is a short street in the Village and has a crook in it—to Anthony Cook's apartment in West Twelfth. Walking them, Tony had vague qualms. Probably, he should have tried harder to keep his mind on what she was telling him. Understandably, it was important to her. But so were other things, he thought, as he climbed the stairs to his apartment.

Tomorrow—today, that is—when we drive into the country, I'll listen more carefully. And, of course, we'll both have our clothes on.

2

IT HAD BEEN a pleasant Sunday in the country. It had not been perceptibly cooler; the relative coolness of the country is, at least during daylight hours, largely an illusion. Heat does not, to be sure, glare up from grass as from pavements. Air, not handcuffed by tall buildings, does move a little more freely when it is inclined to move at all. On that July Sunday, even in Putnam County, the air had been content to sit—heavily. But it had been cool at the inn where they lunched.

Tony had brought up the matter of her embryonic career as an actress, but she had brushed it down again. "We've been over that," Rachel had said. "I told you all I know about it last night. You didn't really listen. Anyway, it's sort of secret, I think."

He insisted he had listened. At any rate until he was distracted. Which, on the whole, was as much her fault as his.

"All right," Rachel said then, "we distract each other. And, all right, I'm glad we do. That looks like a nice, peaceful road."

They had taken the nice peaceful road, which was narrow and curving and up and down. It was also tree-shaded, and Tony turned off the air conditioning in the rented Chevy and opened the windows. "What's that funny smell?" Rachel had asked. Tony told her the funny smell was air and, since they were passing a pasture, a little cow.

They had had to go back to a main highway to reach the inn, and then the air was primarily exhaust fumes and Tony turned the air conditioning on again and closed the windows. Lunch was admirable, and they did not hurry over it. Asked, Rachel was sure she would not have to go off to Hollywood. "As sure as I am about any of it," she said.

They had started back early, to "avoid the rush." The rush of homing New Yorkers joined them. When they were still almost twenty-five miles from Manhattan, a raging thunderstorm also joined them. The wipers fought against a sheet of water. Thunder bombarded them and lightning tore holes in the sky. Rachel said "Ow!" at intervals, and Tony, after confirming her interjection once or twice, said nothing at all. The Saw Mill River Parkway, which floods rather eagerly, had only started to flood when they had finished with it. They were on the Henry Hudson when the rain stopped. They left the Henry Hudson at Ninety-sixth Street—the West Side Highway being closed—and went on down West End Avenue, which after a while became Eleventh. When they turned off that onto Twenty-third Street, the sun was coming out.

They left the car at the rental garage and found

a cab to take them to Hugo's on Sixth Avenue. Now that it had stopped raining, there were plenty of cabs. It was only a little after nine when they climbed the stairs to Rachel's apartment.

"No, Tony," Rachel said, when he reached toward her. "I've got an appointment at the crack of dawn. Of course you can kiss me good night. No, Tony. *No.* Go home, Tony. I promise I won't go to Hollywood. Anyway, who does anymore? *No,* Tony. And your gun's jabbing into me. And I won't forget to fasten the chain. Good night, Tony. It was a lovely day. Good *night.*"

I don't think she's really cross with me, Tony thought at his desk in the Homicide South squad room at a little after eight on Monday morning. We did keep our clothes on all day, but we've done that before, now and then. And this acting job of hers, if there is an acting job, won't take her out of town. That time, somebody flew her over to Paris on a modeling job because they wanted an authentic Eiffel Tower background—that time was bad enough.

There were reports to type, in triplicate. There were always reports to type. It was lucky, Tony thought, that he had elected a typing course in high school. Did anybody write longhand anymore? "Held. Chg. involuntary manslaughter." Nobody was ever going to keep firearms out of the hands of butterfingered idiots. Nobody was trying, thanks to the National Rifle Association and a misreading of the Constitution of the United States. Hadn't anybody ever thought of banning the manufacture of ammunition, except for the use of the armed forces and law-enforcement officers? Let the killers kill with what cartridges they had until they ran out of them. Try to catch them, of course. Oh, supply ammunition to forest rangers and game wardens. Otherwise the country will be overrun by deer. Like the three does we saw yesterday, grazing with the cows. Of course, people would try to make their own gunpowder. There were, he'd read, illegal whiskey stills still working in the mountains of the Carolinas. Probably in New York mountains, too. A good many people trying to home-brew gunpowder would blow themselves up. And people would hit each other over the head with empty revolvers and rifles.

He wound reports out of his typewriter and wound new forms in, along with carbon paper. He typed reports. People had been killed on Saturday, but not very interestingly. Which was a hell of a way to think about violent death. But detectives, also, can be bored. Revolted, but at the same time bored. Perhaps, if one stayed at it long enough, not even revolted, not even angry. I hope I retire before I get like that, Anthony Cook thought.

It was eleven-thirty before he got his first call of the day—knifing in a Washington Street tenement hallway near the southern tip of the island of Manhattan. Tony took Detective (3rd gr.) Samuel Oscar Sanders—known, rather obviously, as "S.O.S."—with him.

The tenement on Washington Street was ancient and ugly and five stories tall. There were two police cruise cars and a precinct squad car parked in front of it. One of the cruisers had had to double-park. There was an Armenian restaurant on the ground floor. A man in a chef's apron, not very clean, was standing in the doorway of the restaurant, looking out.

A patrolman in uniform came out of a narrow doorway on one side of the restaurant entrance and went to the double-parked cruiser, which had been talking to itself in a raspy monotone. It stopped talking, and the patrolman talked. "Damn it, we're beginning to get flies," he said. He got out of the cruiser and came to the squad car, which Sanders had had to double-park behind the cruiser. "Have to ask you to move along," the patrolman said. "Can't stop here, blocking traffic the way you are."

"Homicide," Sanders said.

The patrolman said, "O.K., Mac. Second floor. Still lying there, the stiff is. Where the hell the van is, we're trying to find out. M.E.'s been here and the lab boys and all. Cadaver's still lying there. Come on if you're coming."

They followed him up a narrow flight of stairs. Blood had flowed down the stairs, but they could, with care, edge around it. The blood was dry, now. The body of a dark-haired youngish man was sprawled on the landing. It wasn't bleeding anymore. A door off the landing stood open. Tony Cook edged around the body, and Sanders followed him. There was another uniformed man in the room—the small, cluttered room—the open door led to. There were also two men in civilian clothes, with gold-colored shields pinned to their jackets. Cook and Sanders pinned their own shields on. Regulations require that shields be visible at the scene of a crime. Tony knew one of the detectives from the precinct squad. Tony said, "Hi, Frank," to Detective (1st gr.) Francis Pergotilli. He got a "Hi" back.

"Stuck him with a butcher knife," Pergotilli said. "Just happened to be taking the knife around the corner to be sharpened, according to her first story. Nineteen, she says she is. Says he tried to rape her. Trouble with that is, they've been shacking up for damn near a year, and we've found half a dozen people who don't mind swearing to it. People who live in this dump.

Over at the station house now, they are. So's the girl. Marcella Little, she says her name is. No place we can find around here sharpens knives. Probably coming clean right now, Marcella is. Boyfriend playing around, so she stuck a knife in him."

"Pretty much cleaned up, way it sounds," Tony said.

"Except for that damn—well, about time." The last was to two men in white uniforms who were coming up the stairs. They stopped at the landing, and one of them unrolled a furled canvas stretcher.

"Busy morning," one of the white-uniformed men said to Detective Pergotilli. "Another one of those goddamn stair jobs," he said to the other man, who was trying to spread the stretcher out beside the body and finding there wasn't enough room for it.

"You're lucky it isn't on the fifth floor," Pergotilli told them.

Tony got the name of the victim and said he couldn't see the point of sitting in on it at the precinct station house. "Guess you've got it pretty well sewed up," he said, and Pergotilli said he guessed they had.

Homicide frequently gets called in on killings the precinct squad has wrapped up, or is about to wrap up. And there are almost always butcher knives hysterical people can lay hands on. No, Sanders didn't mind writing it up for them. He wasn't in any hurry about lunch. Tony Cook wasn't particularly hungry, either. Blood which had flowed down staircases from ripped bodies still made him a little queasy. He likes hamburgers, but likes them only rare. So he ordered a cheese sandwich with his beer. It turned out to be a process cheese and didn't taste of much of anything.

It was a little cooler than it had been the day before. It still wasn't what anybody could call cool. It just wasn't as stifling as it had been Sunday; had been even in the country. He found he was walking toward Gay Street in the Village. Conditioned reflex, he told himself, and turned back toward the office. The present squad room of Homicide South was, at any rate, air-conditioned. Manhattan was really hell in July. And there were still reports to type. In triplicate.

There wasn't much else. A "suspicious death" in an apartment on West Twenty-second. Ferguson was out on it, with Sanders. S.O.S. was finding his neck stuck out.

About two-thirty, Tony was up on his reports and lighted a cigarette. This one he could really smoke. Cigarettes left slanting in ashtrays when fingers are busy are often forgotten and left to smolder out. Of course, those you don't have to count. Some day, probably, he'd have to try one of those filter holders. Only he'd feel rather silly with a holder stuck in his mouth. F.D.R. had got away with it, but F.D.R. was a man who could get away with things.

He agreed with Detective (2nd gr.) Mark Ferguson—now back—that the Yankees were beginning to show signs of life and that it was about time and that nobody would ever see anything like the old Yanks again. And that, yes, it was being a dull day. And that, if all hell broke loose for the four-to-midnight boys, he wouldn't mind too much.

It was after three o'clock, with less than an hour of the shift to go, when Lieutenant Nathan Shapiro came out of his office into the squad room and looked at Tony Cook and used his head to beckon with. Shapiro's long face was set in lines of deep depression, which was the way it was usually set. Perhaps even more so than usual, Tony thought, as he put on his jacket and buttoned it to cover the gun and joined Shapiro at the door.

"You and I," Shapiro said, his voice as depressed as his face, "we always get the lousy ones. Know anything about the advertising racket, Tony? Except that that Rachel girl of yours poses for advertising shots. How is Rachel, by the way?"

Tony said that Rachel was all right and asked about Rose. The sadness diminished in Nathan Shapiro's face. He said that Rose was fine and that he was trying to get her to take a week in the Catskills, where maybe it was cooler than God knew it was in Brooklyn, but that she wouldn't go. "Says if I can stand it, she can. Like her, isn't it?"

Tony agreed that staying in New York in July because her husband had to was very like Rose Shapiro. He added that he didn't know anything about advertising agencies except that Rachel often modeled for them.

They got in a squad car, which had a uniformed man to drive it.

"I didn't suppose you would," Shapiro said, and gave the driver a Madison Avenue address. An address below Forty-second, Tony realized. "Neither do I. I told Bill that, but it didn't do any good. Never does, does it? He keeps on giving us the lousy ones."

"All right, Nate," Tony said. "Because you keep cracking them, maybe."

He was entirely familiar with Shapiro's conviction that Captain William Weigand, commanding, Homicide South, inconsiderately assigns Shapiro cases which involve people entirely alien to Shapiro's experience—cases involving evangelists who preach sermons beyond

Shapiro's ken, people who paint pictures, even people who write novels and publish novels. Beyond Tony's experience, too, except that Rachel knew people of that sort—painters especially—and that he had met some of them with her. They found detectives an alien breed, of course. There was that to keep in mind.

"Suspicious death, precinct boys put it down as," Shapiro said, as the squad car took them uptown, obeying all traffic regulations, stopping at all red lights. "Charlie Fremont's a careful one. Man falls seven floors and squashes on a roof and Charlie gets suspicious. Because, he says, how can you get a window open to fall out of it?"

"Old building, maybe," Tony said. "Ought I to know Fremont?"

"Captain, precinct squad," Shapiro said. "Went out on it himself, apparently. Thorough sort. Always has been. Good cop. Doesn't like to believe what stares him in the face."

"Neither do you," Tony told him, and got "Mmmm" as answer. "The deceased had a name?"

"Name of Bradley," Nathan Shapiro told him. "Firm's Folsom, Akins and Bradley. Something like that, anyway. Here we are."

They were in front of a corner office building a couple of blocks below Forty-second on Madison. It belonged to the setback era, not the more recent straight-up, featureless glass.

"Here we are, Tony," Shapiro repeated. Tony sat for a second or two, looking at the back of the driver's head. Then he said he'd be damned. He didn't say why. After all, Bradley wasn't an unusual name. Probably there were quite a few men named Bradley in the advertising business.

They went into the lobby of the building. A barbershop opened off it, and also a restaurant. It was pleasantly cool in the lobby. The board by the bank of elevators told them that Folsom, Akins & Bradley occupied the twelfth floor. They got into an elevator under a sign that said "Express to 12" and pressed a button marked "12" which glowed its appreciation of their choice.

The car stopped, rather abruptly, and its doors opened on a cubicle which contained a jar partly filled with sand. There were two cigarette butts on top of the sand. There was a small, straight chair against one wall and a small table beside it that held an ashtray. There were no butts in the tray. The door facing them was marked "Folsom, Akins & Bradley." They opened the door and confronted a desk with a very trim young woman behind it. There were deep, leather-covered chairs along the side walls and doors in both of the walls. There was a third door, also closed, behind the receptionist's desk.

Nobody was sitting in any of the chairs.

"Can I help you, gentlemen?" the trim young woman asked them. "Only I'm afraid everybody's canceled every—"

"Police, miss," Shapiro said. He showed her his badge and put it back in his pocket.

"Through that way, Lieutenant," the girl said. "And then straight on to the next-to-last office on your left. That's where they all are."

She had actually looked at his badge, Shapiro thought. Apparently a trim mind went with the trim body. They went through the doorway she had indicated; went along a passage between rows of desks, all except three deserted. Young women were typing at three of the desks. Beyond the desk area—a typists' pool, evidently—they went down a wide corridor, with closed doors on either side of it. The doors had names on them: "Mr. Lawrence," "Mr. Cartwell," "Miss Logan," and a good many others. A plaque on one door was labeled "Art Department." Nearly at the end of the corridor, another short one went off to the right.

A door on the left stood open, and the name on that door was "Mr. Bradley." They went through that doorway, pinning their badges on. They went into a small room and faced a small desk. There was no one behind the desk. A rather wider door stood open behind the desk, and voices came from beyond it. They went through that door into a big corner office. It was not as cool in that office, and a casement window on their left was hinged wide open. A tall, white-haired man stood at the window, his back to the office—and to a large desk with two telephones on it and a high-backed, leather-covered chair behind it. Shapiro said, "Afternoon, Charlie," and the white-haired man turned to face them. He said, "So you got it, Nate. Hell of a long way for the poor son of a bitch."

There were two other men in the room. One wore a sport jacket and had a detective's badge pinned to it. He was sitting in a deep chair, facing toward the desk. The man beside him in an identical chair had wide shoulders, over which a gray suit jacket fitted smoothly. He stood up as Shapiro and Tony went into the room. He had blond hair, cut short, and a tanned squarish face. There was a clipped blond mustache on his upper lip. He wore a white shirt with a button-down collar and a dark red bow tie. It wasn't, Tony thought, a snap-on bow tie. He nodded his head, slowly, at Tony and Nathan Shapiro. There was a waiting, no-comment expression on his tanned face. He did not say anything. He was a tall man, as tall as Tony Cook. He was, Tony thought, probably in his late forties. Tony returned his nod. He also nodded his head, in greeting, at Detective (1st gr.) Ken Latham. Shapiro went over and stood beside Captain Charles Fremont. He looked down. It had been a hell of a long way down.

"Fifth-floor roof," Fremont said. "You can see where he landed." On a section of the fifth-floor roof, above which the setback began, a square of gray canvas was spread. There appeared to be nothing under the canvas.

"Pretty messy," Fremont said.

"Would have been," Nate Shapiro said. "How long ago, Charlie?"

"About an hour. Hour and a half," Fremont told him. "Can't find anybody who saw him fall. Thought somebody over there might be able to fix it, but nope. All hard at work. Not looking out of windows."

"Over there" was the facade of the other rise of the building. There were lighted windows up and down it, and men and women at desks beyond the windows. "That's a 'spire,'" Fremont said. "Building's called 'Twin Spires.' Anyway, we don't know when he fell."

"Around three, probably," the tall, bronzed man said. "We got back about a quarter of. A man was waiting to see him, Miss Kline says. Was in Frank's office only about ten minutes, she says. Man named Langhorn."

They turned back from the window.

"This is Mr. Akins, Nate," Fremont said. "Lieutenant Shapiro, Mr. Akins. Of the Homicide Squad."

Akins said, "Homicide?" There was surprise and question in his voice. "Poor Frank just fell out the window. Tried to get him to have a guardrail put in, but he just laughed at me."

"Probably what happened," Shapiro said. "Just that we're supposed to try to make sure about things. This is Detective Cook, Mr. Akins. Try not to bother you too long. Mr. Bradley was your partner, I take it. Yours and Mr. Folsom's, that is."

"Yes," Akins said. "Mine. Ted Folsom retired several years ago. Founded the agency, Ted did. Folsom and Akins, it was before Frank came in. Now, God knows. Leslie Akins Associates, I guess. But God knows. Few hours ago—a hell of a thing to happen, Lieutenant. One hell of a thing to happen."

He shook his head in a baffled sort of way.

"Few hours ago we were on top of the world," he said. "Just a few lousy hours ago. Damn it to hell. What you say we go into my office? Keep feeling old Frank's still here, somehow."

He led them to a door in the side wall of the office and into another corner office of equal size. Afternoon sun slanted into this one, which was perceptibly cooler than the other had been. The windows in this office were closed. They were, in fact, unopenable, Nate Shapiro noticed. Leslie Akins went to sit behind a wide desk and motioned them toward chairs. Shapiro and Fremont and Tony Cook sat down. Detective Latham had remained in the other office.

"Cooler in here," Akins told them.

He hadn't needed to. The temperature in this air-conditioned office was noticeably lower than in the one which had been Frank Bradley's, now that the door was closed between them. The open window in Bradley's office let in the city's steaming air—the city's lung-clogging air.

"Much cooler," Shapiro agreed.

"Whole building's cooler than Frank wants—" The present tense stopped him for a moment. "Than poor Frank wanted his office," Akins said. "Had to have the duct shut off when he joined us. And workable windows put in. Cost quite a bit, actually. The people who own the building let out a squawk, and we had to fork over half of it. They still yelled. Something about upsetting the whole balance of the building, whatever they meant by that. But we're good tenants, with a long lease. So—"

"Mr. Bradley objected to air conditioning?"

"Had a thing about it, Lieutenant. A lot of sinus trouble, Frank had. Had some idea that air conditioning is bad for sinuses. Don't know where he got it. Be the other way around, you'd think, wouldn't you? Air conditioning filters the muck out of the air. Some of it, anyway. But there was no arguing Frank out of it. People get notions, don't they?"

Nathan Shapiro agreed that people got notions. "These sinus attacks Mr. Bradley had," Shapiro said. "Ever make him dizzy?"

"If they did, he never mentioned it. Oh. I see what you're getting at. Low sill on that window in there. As I said, I tried to get him to have a guardrail put in. But no, he never said anything about getting dizzy. Never talked about his health, actually. Except for this sinus thing. Always seemed fit to me. In damn good condition for his age, I'd have said."

"We have to check out all possibilities," Shapiro told the man who sat so erect behind his desk. "About how old was Mr. Bradley?"

"Fifty. Around there, anyway. Had his own agency for ten years or so, before he and I joined up. After

Ted Folsom retired, that was. Ted had been creative executive, you see. Left a hole when he stepped out. Frank filled it for us."

Shapiro said he saw, which wasn't entirely true. Creative executive? As usual, Nathan thought, Bill Weigand's thrown me in out of my depth. This time, I don't even know the terminology.

"When was this, Mr. Akins? When you and Mr. Bradley became associated. Became partners. It is a partnership, I gather. Not a corporation?"

"Partnership, yes. We've never incorporated. Three years ago, Lieutenant—or nearly. Three years come October, actually. He brought several accounts with him, of course. One big one. Hopkins Industries, that was. The cosmetic people, you know. Soaps. Shampoos. Antiperspirants. Face creams. That sort of thing. Got a new product coming out, as a matter of fact. Toothpaste. Call it 'Dazzle.' For that 'dazzling smile.' Frank gave them the name for it. TV spots, starting in September. With Lusterglow going piggyback."

"Lusterglow?"

"Shampoo, Lieutenant. 'Restore youth's luster to your hair.' Aimed at women in their forties and fifties. Women's magazines. What are left of them. And TV spots, of course. Piggyback, some of them. Straight thirty seconds on others."

It didn't get any simpler for Nate Shapiro. Nor did it seem to be getting them anywhere, like how Frank Bradley had come to fall out of a window to a messy death.

"Thirty seconds doesn't sound like much time," Fremont said, not advancing matters.

"We can cram a lot into thirty seconds," Akins said. "Have to, at what the networks charge. Up to a

28

hundred and fifty thousand, full network, prime time."

Nate said "Dollars?" involuntarily. But he knew Akins had meant a hundred and fifty thousand dollars. For half a minute he just found it hard to believe.

"Suppose we get back to today," Nathan Shapiro said.

3

UNTIL IT ENDED as it did, the day had been like any other day, Akins told them. Akins himself had shown a couple of renderings to clients. And—

"Renderings?" Shapiro asked.

"Mock-ups of ads," Akins said. "For magazine advertisements, Lieutenant. Layouts. Illustrations here. Text there. With simulated type, of course. But the text typed out for them to O.K. The one for Texton went over big. Four-color job. Mostly photographs of this new synthetic of theirs. Folds and folds of it. Hell of a layout. I'll say that for Wally. Damn sincere text. Their ad manager gobbled it up. Chris Rogers. Got it around here somewhere—if you'd like to see it?"

"Don't bother, Mr. Akins. Some other time, maybe. You showed this rendering when? This morning?"

"Around ten. Didn't take long. Rogers knows a good thing when he sees it. Not like Birnham. Cranky old bastard, Nat Birnham is. Of course, his program'll run to three or four million. Naturally wants to make sure it'll sell cars. He's Mini-Motors, you know."

Akins did not merely drop names—probably all of them irrelevant. He hurled names. Nate Shapiro cringed slightly under the impact. He repeated "Cars?"

"Mini-Motors. Little beetles, they make. Make in Japan, actually. Can't call them 'beetles' of course. Took an hour, damn near, to make Nat see why. That Volks agency's got a genius handling the account. Have to admit that, I guess. Yes, sure have to give them that."

"That was today? That you showed this—rendering—to Mr. Birnham?"

"Around ten-thirty until lunchtime. Right after Texton—I told you Texton snapped theirs up, didn't I? No sweat with Rogers. Old Nat was—oh, all right— a different kettle of fish. Has been for the last couple of years. Hard man to deal with. But then—fifteen percent of maybe four million a year—well, there you are, if you get what I mean."

Nate got what he meant, or thereabouts. He'd thought agencies got only ten percent. No, that was what authors' agents got. Agents for painters got a lot more, but they had to run galleries. Information you had to pick up on one case was no damn good on the next. Not as long as Bill Weigand kept throwing the odd ones at him. Probably next time he'd need a course in nuclear physics.

"Mr. Bradley," Nate said. "Any idea what he was doing today?"

"In his office," Akins said. "This morning, that is. Trying to work out a bug for Birnham, I guess. Way we'd planned it, anyway. All right, we knew we didn't have it in the rendering I showed the old grouch today. Amelia'll probably know."

"Amelia?"

"Amelia Kline. She's his secretary. Was, anyway. You'll have to ask her, Lieutenant." He looked at the watch on his wrist. "If she hasn't gone for the day."

Shapiro looked at his own watch. It was a quarter of five.

"We'd like her to wait around for a while," he told Leslie Akins. "Will you see—"

But Akins had already switched on his intercom. It said, "Yes, Mr. Akins," in a rasping but female voice.

"Amelia happen to be in there with you, Sue? If she is, the police say they'd like to have a word with her. Ask her to stick around for a while, will you?"

"Of course, Mr. Akins. She's—well, sort of broken up, you know."

"We all are," Akins said. His voice, which had had an almost sprightly tone when he had talked of Texton and of Birnham's Mini-Motors, moderated to a texture more appropriate. "Think she'd like a brandy or something?"

There was a brief pause. Then, "She says not, Mr. Akins. We've both had coffee sent in. She'll be here when they want to talk to her."

Akins said, "Fine, Sue. And you might stick around too, if you don't mind."

"Certainly, Mr. Akins."

"Sue Perkins," Akins said to Shapiro. "My secretary. Amelia's in there with her. Taking it hard, apparently. Been working with Frank since he joined us."

"Which was nearly three years ago, you said, Mr. Akins. Bringing several accounts with him. About those accounts. They'll stay with the firm?"

Akins spread his hands. He shrugged. Then he said, "No reason why not, I hope. Up to the clients, of course. You can't ever tell about clients, Lieutenant.

Gee whiz, some of them. Go skittering off. But I think the accounts Frank brought with him will stick around. We've done a good job for them. Frank was good. Damn good. But he's not the only good man around. Take over the creative end myself, if it comes to that. Frank handled it the last couple of years. No reason I can't take it on."

Nathan Shapiro nodded his head, in acceptance of the assertion that Leslie Akins was as creative as anyone else. Nathan had supposed that creation was the province of Jehovah, but it appeared that He could delegate.

"You said you and Mr. Bradley 'got back' about a quarter of three," Shapiro said. "From where, Mr. Akins? Lunch, I suppose? And that a Mr. Langhorn was waiting to see him."

"Yes, Lieutenant. We had lunch at the Ad Lib, as we often did unless we were splurging for clients, if you see what I mean. Little place on Thirty-fifth. Easy walking distance, and Frank did say he had to get back because he had an appointment with Langhorn. Pain in the ass, Langhorn's been. But more Frank's ass than mine."

Nathan merely raised eyebrows above his melancholy eyes.

"Writer," Akins said. "Frank had an option on a book of his. Oh, assigned to the firm when Frank joined me, of course. No use to us, as it's turned out. Been making a nuisance of himself, Langhorn has. Claims Frank gypped him. But he took Frank's offer for the option—a thousand, I think it was. And the option's clear enough. TV rights in perpetuity if we take it up. Pretty academic, as it's turned out. I think Frank had a nibble before we joined up. But nothing came of it. And nothing has since. Langhorn made noises about suing, but he wouldn't have had a prayer, our lawyers say."

Nathan said that perpetuity seemed like a long time. He said that Langhorn probably didn't like Frank Bradley much, if he thought Bradley had gypped him.

"Hated his guts, probably," Akins said. "Oh, all right. Could be old Frank made what might have been a shrewd deal, if anything had come of it. Some authors do better. Get paid for each show. And don't have to write the scripts. Also get screen credit. 'Character created by Joe Zilch.' That sort of thing. Frank was to pay a flat five thousand. On top of the option money. All right, Langhorn should have had an agent. Or read the contract before he signed it. Water under the bridge, anyway. And, as it turned out, no water."

Nathan raised his eyebrows again.

"No sponsor," Akins said. "We tried it on a few clients, but no soap. Costs one hell of a lot, a series like that does. Scriptwriters, actors, cameramen, light men, directors and assistant directors—whole thing runs to quite a lot. And network time on top of it. Got to sell the product, but big."

Nathan said he saw, and again with only partial truth. He decided to go back to something simpler.

"At lunch," he said. "You and Mr. Bradley had a drink or two, maybe?"

"I had a couple of dry manhattans," Akins said. "Frank had a couple of martinis. Could be he had three. We were going over things and I didn't pay much attention. You getting at something, Lieutenant?"

"Whether Mr. Bradley had enough to drink to make him a little—well, wobbly?"

"So he'd lose balance and fall out the window? No, I shouldn't think so. He seemed steady enough when we were walking back. Nothing to show he was feeling the drinks. Anyway, about what we usually have when we lunch together. Of course, sometimes drinks hit you harder one day than they do another. And a muggy day like this—well, nobody's up to par. And old Frank just had a salad for lunch. Did, sometimes. Always a light eater, at lunch anyway. I suppose it's possible he was feeling a couple of drinks. All I can say is, he didn't show it. Not to me, anyway. But—you wouldn't have any more investigating to do, if that was the way it was, would you? Just—just accidental death. Damn tragic thing, but there we'd be, wouldn't we?"

Leslie Akins could stretch the obvious out to considerable length, Shapiro thought. But he agreed that that was where they would be. He said they might have a word with Miss Kline and let her go home—that, after all, she'd had a shock.

"We all have," Akins said. "In here, Lieutenant? I've got a few things to clear up."

"Perhaps her office," Shapiro said, and he and Tony Cook and Captain Charles Fremont stood up. Akins remained sitting, very upright, behind his wide desk. "Just go through Frank's office," he told them. "I'll see she's right along."

They went through the connecting doorway between Akins's office and the one which had been Frank Bradley's. Detective Latham was standing by the open window through which Bradley had fallen. The window, Nathan Shapiro noticed, did have a low sill. Not more than a couple of feet above the floor. Akins had been right in urging his partner to have a guardrail put across the window. An easy enough window to fall out of, particularly if a couple, or three, drinks had left you a little woozy. They'd have left me that way, Nate thought. And also with a growling stomach. But probably men in the advertising business got used to drinks in the middle of the day and didn't notice them. I don't know a damn thing about people like Akins and Bradley, Nate thought. I don't even know their habits.

"Looks like maybe I was crying wolf," Fremont said. "Nothing to bring you guys in on, Nate. But it just—well, didn't feel kosher. Just—accidental death?"

"Could be," Nathan said.

"Anyway," Fremont said, "Ken and I may as well get along back to the station house."

"Sure," Nate said. "Tony and I'll poke around a little more. Probably not come up with anything."

Fremont said, "O.K.," and he and Detective Latham went out of the office. There were two doors in the wall opposite, and they used the one which opened directly on the corridor. That door had no name lettered on it, only the room number. Shapiro and Cook used the other door, which let them into Amelia Kline's office. There was nobody in the small office.

"All right, Tony," Shapiro said. "What're you keeping bottled up?"

Tony was not aware that he had showed signs of bottling anything up. Sometimes Nate seemed to have second sight, or something.

"Probably nothing," Tony said. "Only, Saturday night Rachel told me she was maybe going to get an acting part in a movie. TV kind of movie—something she called a pilot. And that a Mr. Bradley had offered it to her. Maybe another Mr.—"

He stopped because the door from the corridor opened and a small young woman, with short black hair and a small, beautifully designed face came into the room. Her full lips trembled a little, Tony thought. He also thought she had been crying.

"Miss Kline?" Nathan Shapiro said. "We'll try not to keep you too long. My name's Shapiro. Police lieutenant. This is Detective Cook. Probably this bad thing has made you—well, a little shaky."

"I'm all right," she said. "It's a dreadful thing, but I'm all right."

She crossed the room rather, Nathan thought, as if she were feeling her way across it. She sat at her desk. There was only one other chair in the small office. Shapiro pulled it toward the desk and sat on it. Tony stood, his back against the wall.

"About this afternoon," Shapiro said. "Mr. Akins says he and Mr. Bradley got back from lunch about a quarter of three. Way you remember it, Miss Kline?"

"Yes," she said. "It was about then. Fr—Mr. Bradley went directly into his office. I mean, not through here. It was—oh, about ten of three when he told me to have Mr. Langhorn go in."

"Told you on the intercom?"

"Yes. Mr. Langhorn's appointment wasn't until three, actually. But he was early. Got to the reception desk about twenty of. I said Mr. Bradley hadn't come back from lunch yet but that I was expecting him any moment and that Mr. Langhorn could come in here and wait, if he wanted to. So he came in. Sat on that chair you're sitting on, Lieutenant. Shapiro, you said your name is? I'm—I'm all confused."

"Shapiro, yes. Nathan Shapiro. It's quite natural you should be confused, Miss Kline. Just take it easy. Mr. Langhorn just sat here and waited?"

"He fidgeted a lot. The chair wasn't big enough for him, I guess. He's a big man, you know."

Shapiro didn't know. He said, "Mr. Langhorn had been in to see Mr. Bradley before?"

"Several times, Lieutenant. Last spring—well, it

seemed like he came in almost every day. Sometimes—oh, just barged in."

"Mr. Bradley always saw Mr. Langhorn when he came in? Even when he barged in?"

"Yes. Oh, sometimes he'd say, 'God, not *again.*' Something like that. But he always saw him."

"Have you any idea what he came to see Mr. Bradley about?"

"About the rights to a book Mr. Langhorn had written," she said. "The performance rights. Television. Mr. Bradley owned them. That is, the firm does now, of course. Mr. Langhorn wasn't satisfied with the terms of the contract. Thought—said he thought, anyway—that they weren't fair. Which wasn't true, of course. Frank—I mean Mr. Bradley—is always fair. The fairest—"

She did not finish. She spread her hands flat on the desk in front of her and put her forehead down on them. Shapiro waited. After a few seconds, he said, "Just take it easy, Miss Kline. I realize this is hard for you."

She was sobbing, quietly. Her slim shoulders moved with her sobs. After a little, she said, "I'm sorry. Terribly sorry." Her voice was choked. Then she said, in the same muffled voice, "Almost three years. Would have been three in—and now it's all—like a light turned off." She lifted her head. She sat straight in her chair. After she had cleared her throat, her voice was steady again. It was a light, clear voice.

"I don't know why I'm acting like this," Amelia Kline said. "It's really ridiculous, Lieutenant Shapiro. It's only that Mr. Bradley was a fine man. A very fine man. And I've got so used to working for him. I'm dreadfully sorry. I don't know what you're thinking of me."

"That you've had a very bad experience, Miss Kline. One that I'm making you go through again. If it's too much for you, we can—well, it can wait until tomorrow." He paused. He said, "I suppose."

She shook her head. There was something like defiance in the movement of her head. Shapiro did not think it was defiance of him.

"Mr. Bradley told you to have Mr. Langhorn come in," he said. "He went in? About what time did you say?"

"About ten minutes of three."

"And closed the door after him, I suppose. So that you couldn't hear what they talked about."

"Yes. No. Of course I couldn't. Anyway, I was busy. Typing. A long memo to Mr. Parker. He's the executive on the Hopkins Industries account—one of the accounts Mr. Bradley controlled. Had overall charge of. About the general ideas the copywriter was to try to get over."

Shapiro said he saw. He was getting used to assuring people he saw what he didn't see. The words were getting dry in his mouth.

"Was Mr. Langhorn very long in Mr. Bradley's office, Miss Kline?"

"Only about ten minutes."

"He came out this way? Through this office?"

"Yes."

"How did he look?"

She didn't know what he meant.

"Angry? Upset? As if, say, he and Mr. Bradley had been having an argument?"

"Mr. Langhorn always looks angry," she said. "When I've seen him, anyway. And he did sound angry, I guess."

"After he came out? Said something angrily to you?"

"Oh, no. Not to me. I don't suppose he even knew I was here. To Mr. Bradley. Spoke back in to him as he was closing the door. What he said was, 'You'll find out.' No. 'You'll sure as hell find out.' And then he closed the door. Slammed it, almost."

"Did you hear Mr. Bradley answer him? When Langhorn said that Mr. Bradley would find out. Would sure as hell find out."

"I didn't hear anything. Just the door banging."

"And Mr. Langhorn didn't say anything to you?"

"He just—went out."

"As if he were in a hurry?"

"He always seemed in a hurry whenever I saw him. As if he were running after something. He's a writer, of course. Even some of our copywriters act— oh, strangely. As if they were running after things and not catching them."

Nathan supposed they did; supposed, also, that this tense, shaken young woman knew more about them than he did. The writer with whom he had had the nearest to a personal contact had been dead when he saw her. To Amelia Kline's generalization, he merely nodded his head. Then he said, "Go on, Miss Kline. Mr. Langhorn went out. In a hurry. Then?"

Then she had gone back to typing the memo to Mr. Parker. She had almost finished it when the telephone rang. The call was for Mr. Bradley. His wife was calling. "At least, she said, 'Mr. Bradley, please. This is Mrs. Bradley.'"

"You say she said she was Mrs. Bradley. I take it you didn't recognize her voice?"

"She'd never called before, Lieutenant. Not since

I've been Mr. Bradley's secretary. Which has been since he joined the firm. Three years, and now—" Her voice seemed to catch in her throat. But when she went on, her voice was light and clear and steady. There was strain, however, in the tiny muscles around her dark brown eyes.

"I called Mr. Bradley on the intercom," she said. "I said that Mrs. Bradley was calling and should I put her through. I never put anybody through without asking him. It was always the way he wanted it. Sometimes, of course, he'd be in the middle of something and not want to be interrupted."

She stopped, as if she had finished. After a few seconds, Shapiro said, "Go on, Miss Kline. Did Mr. Bradley say to put his wife on?"

"He didn't—" Her voice faltered again. "He didn't say anything. I said, 'Mr. Bradley? Mr. *Bradley?*' and then I thought he'd probably gone into Mr. Akins's office. They went back and forth quite a bit, and I told Mrs. Bradley that her husband seemed to have stepped—to have stepped out of his office and that if she'd hold on I'd try to find him. She said, all right, she'd hold on. So I went into his office. He wasn't there and—and the door to Mr. Akins's office was closed. But the window was wide open. Wider open than I'd ever seen it. So—oh, I don't know why. I don't know *why*—so I went over to the window. And, I looked down, Lieutenant. *I looked down.*"

Then her slim body began to shake. The movement of her body was convulsive, and Shapiro got up from his chair and began to reach toward her. But she stiffened her body, stiffened the trembling out of it, and shook her head. Shapiro sat down again. For a long moment, silence seemed to congeal in the room.

"Try not to think about it, Miss Kline," Shapiro said and thought that not even he had ever said such meaningless words.

She merely looked at him. Looked at him, he thought, as he deserved to be looked at.

"I'm sorry," Nathan Shapiro said. "You knew it was Mr. Bradley?"

She nodded her head, the movement stiff. Her hands trembled on the surface of her desk and he thought she was about to lift them to cover her staring eyes. She did not.

"Yes," she said. "I knew it was Frank. Don't ask me how I knew. Right away, I knew it was Frank. And I knew he was dead. I knew of course he was dead. I—"

Suddenly, she lifted her hands up, but it was not to cover her eyes—not to shut the now ugly world out from in front of them. Her hands went up to cover her mouth, both of them pressing hard against it. Then she was up from behind her desk and running out of the little office. She did not close the door behind her. They could hear the click of her heels as she ran down the corridor.

"A bad thing to see," Nathan Shapiro said. "Even when you see it from a distance, as she did."

"Yes," Tony Cook said. "And not something you get used to, is it? Really get used to. I had a bad one this morning. Just before lunchtime. I didn't want much lunch. And God knows we see enough of them. Cut-up people, smashed-up people. And for a kid like her."

"Yes, Tony. And I made her remember what she saw. Not an easy trade, ours, Tony. And Bradley was more to her than a boss, pretty obviously, wouldn't you say? I wonder if the precinct boys have got in touch with this wife of his—this widow of his."

Tony Cook could only shrug his shoulders.

"Yes," Nate Shapiro said. "Something we'll have to find out. Quite a few things we'll have to find out, aren't there? Bradley didn't have to come through here to get into his office. Door directly to the corridor. Have to find out if it was kept locked, of course. Or whether anybody could just walk in. We'll ask Miss Kline about that when she gets back."

"If," Tony said. "Could be—"

He stopped, because they could both hear again the click of heels on the corridor tile. But it was not Amelia Kline who came into the small office.

She did not really come into the office. She stopped in the doorway and looked at them, hostility in cold gray eyes. She was, at a guess, in her middle thirties, at least ten years older than Amelia Kline. Her brown hair was cut short; she wore a black dress, with white at the collar and cuffs; she made it look like a uniform. She said, "What have you two been doing to that poor child?" There was hostility in her voice as in her eyes. There was also accusation.

"We're police officers," said Nathan Shapiro. He gave their names. "We're trying to find out what happened here this afternoon. To do that, we have to ask questions. Miss—?"

"You made her sick. Terribly sick."

"What she saw made her sick," Shapiro said. "Remembering it made her sick. She looked down from the window. What she saw wasn't pleasant. The sort of thing that does make people sick, Miss—?"

"All right, Perkins. Sue Perkins. Couldn't you two men see how upset she was? I made her go home. Promise to get a taxi and go home. Not stay here and let the two of you hammer at her. It is bad enough for her without that. She was—very fond of Frank Bradley. And she's really a child. Couldn't you two see that?"

"She's very young," Shapiro said. "Vulnerable. Yes. And in love with Bradley, wasn't she?"

"I don't know. How would I know? Oh, perhaps. What has that to do with anything? With his falling out of a window?"

"I don't know," Shapiro said. "Nothing, probably. You're Mr. Akins's secretary, Miss Perkins?"

"Mrs. Perkins, actually. Not that that matters either. You made her go back over things, I suppose. Remember it all over again. And made the poor child sick. At her stomach, if you want to know. Terribly. I happened to be in the washroom when she ran in. Her face—her face was dreadful. Then she was sick."

"Yes. And we're sorry. We're both sorry. And probably you were right in urging her to go home. Where does she live, by the way?"

"Over in the Murray Hill area. East Thirties. You going to follow her over there and—ask her a lot more questions? Hammer away at her again?"

"Not unless we have to, Mrs. Perkins. Perhaps, now that you're here, you can help us out on a few points."

"I don't know what they'd be. He and Mr. Akins went out to lunch. Probably had several drinks. Mr. Bradley was—well, a little drunk, probably. Just—staggered out of that damn window he always kept open."

"That may have been the way it happened, of course. Did Mr. Bradley often have too many drinks at lunch, Mrs. Perkins? Noticeably, I mean?"

"They all drink their lunches, Lieutenant. It's the kind of people they are. And clients, especially the ones from out of town, expect to be given long, sort of lavish lunches. Sometimes Mr. Akins doesn't get back from lunch until after four."

"I see," Nathan Shapiro said, and sounded to himself like a stuck phonograph record. "But today, I under-

44

stood from Mr. Akins, he and Mr. Bradley weren't taking a client to lunch. Just the two of them, I thought. To a restaurant called the Ad Lib. And they got back before three. Did you see Mr. Bradley after they got back from lunch, Mrs. Perkins?"

"No. Why should I?"

"You did see Mr. Akins, I suppose. He was—well, all right?"

"Of course he was."

"Quite his usual self?"

"Why, yes. Of course he was."

"Not upset? Anything like that?"

She didn't know what he was getting at. Mr. Akins had been just as he always was. "He was dictating some letters when the poor child began pounding on the door. We'd just started."

"Miss Kline, you mean? She pounded on the door?"

"After she'd—seen Mr. Bradley. To tell Mr. Akins what had happened."

"And you and Mr. Akins went into the other office? And—saw what Miss Kline had seen?"

"He did, I guess. I—well, I had too much sense, Lieutenant."

"Wise of you, of course. Nasty thing to see. You say Mr. Akins was just as he usually was when they came back from lunch. You think Mr. Bradley wasn't? That perhaps he'd had a little too much to drink? But you say you didn't see him after they came back."

"All right. I was just guessing, I suppose. Trying to guess at what probably happened. Think of an explanation of such an awful thing."

"Yes. Quite a natural thing to do, Mrs. Perkins. Tell me about Mr. Bradley, will you?"

"What about him?"

"Oh, anything. What he looked like. What kind of

man he was. Anything you think of which might help us."

"Well, he wasn't a big man. Rather good-looking, I guess you'd say. Wore sport jackets, most of the time. Sport shirts too, sometimes. Even here in the office. Seemed, oh, friendly enough, I suppose you'd say. I didn't see much of him, actually. And I'm not the one to ask about him. If you go snooping around, as apparently you're going to, you'll find out why, I guess. People talk, you know."

"All right. If we're going to find out anyway. Is there some special reason you're not the right person to ask about Mr. Bradley?"

She hesitated.

"Why don't you go over and sit at the desk, Mrs. Perkins? No point in standing up. We may have one or two more things to ask you about. What will these people have to talk about if we go on snooping around? As I'm afraid we'll be doing."

"All right. Mr. Bradley had my husband fired, if you want to know. And it wasn't fair. Leon's just as good as any of them. And he'd been here for years."

"Here at the agency?"

"Of course. He was a copywriter here, and everybody thought he was a good one. A very good one. Everybody except Mr. Bradley. As soon as he came here, he started finding fault with everything Leon did."

"And had Mr. Perkins discharged," Shapiro said. "This was some time ago, Mrs. Perkins? And is your husband unemployed now?"

"Of course not. But he's working for about half what he's worth. And so I have to keep on working. But I didn't push him out of the window. And Leon didn't. If that's what you're getting at."

Nathan Shapiro said he wasn't getting at anything. He said he didn't know that anybody had pushed Frank Bradley out the window Bradley had insisted on having installed because he thought air conditioning was bad for his sinuses.

"You say Mr. Bradley wasn't a big man, Mrs. Perkins. Was he a very small man? Is that what you meant?"

The autopsy report would answer that, of course. But you pick up what you can as you go along, subject to further verification.

"No, not all that small. About as tall as most men, I guess. Only he was very thin. Slight, I suppose you'd call it. And in the winter he'd sometimes stay away from the office for two or three days at a time. Because of this sinus trouble, I guess."

"And he'd call in and say he was taking the day off? Or have somebody else call in for him? His wife, perhaps? Call Miss Kline, I suppose?"

"I don't know," Sue Perkins said. "I guess so."

She guessed at a good many things, Nathan thought.

"I don't know about his wife," she said. "Apparently she stays out somewhere on Long Island most of the time. They have a house out there. At least, that's what he told Amelia. They've got a big apartment up in the East Fifties somewhere, Amelia told me once. A perfectly beautiful apartment, she says. But not air conditioned."

"Possibly the reason Mrs. Bradley stays out on Long Island," Shapiro said. "Miss Kline described Mr. Bradley's apartment to you, I take it. As if she'd been there, Mrs. Perkins?"

"Can't you leave that poor child alone, Lieutenant?" The shrillness, the animosity had come back into her voice.

"We can't leave anybody alone," Shapiro told her. "Not yet, anyway. Do you know a Mr. Langhorn, Mrs. Perkins?"

"Of him. Some writer or other. Trying to make a nuisance of himself, Mr. Akins told me once. And if he ever tried to see Mr. Akins, Mr. Akins was to be out of town."

"Did he ever? Try to see Mr. Akins?"

Not that she remembered.

"Do you suppose Mr. Langhorn's address is around here somewhere? And his first name?"

It might, she thought, be in Amelia Kline's files. All right, she'd have a look. She also had a rather pointed look at the watch on her wrist.

She got up from the desk and went to a small file index. She flicked through it.

Langhorn's first name was Timothy. His address was on Morton Street.

She did not go back to the chair behind the desk. She stood and looked at Lieutenant Nathan Shapiro. "Do you want me anymore?" she said. "To sign a statement, or something? Because it's way after five, and the office closes at five."

"No," Shapiro said. "And we won't need a statement. Not now, anyway. Thank you for your cooperation, Mrs. Perkins."

She made a "Hup!" which was a little like a snort, and went out of the office. They could hear her resolute heel clicks as she took the few steps to her own office. They heard the closing of her office door. There was resolution in the closing of the door. It almost amounted to a bang.

"She doesn't like us much, does she?" Tony Cook said.

Shapiro said that a lot of people didn't like policemen much and that probably everybody who worked at the agency had gone home.

"But we don't," Tony said.

Nathan Shapiro said he guessed they didn't.

4

It was, as Leslie Akins had said it would be, only a short walk to the restaurant called "Ad Lib." Tony Cook did not walk it fast. For one thing, it was hot—oppressively hot, as one came out of an acutely air-conditioned building. For another thing, as he had told Nate Shapiro, there was at least an even chance that Ad Lib was open only for lunch. It was not in an area for much of a dinner trade. But it would do no harm, as Shapiro had pointed out when he got into the squad car and gave Langhorn's address to the uniformed driver, to check it out.

Ad Lib was open. Its entrance on Thirty-fifth Street was two steps down and unobtrusive. Ad Lib did not reach out for customers. Customers could find it. At twenty of six that Monday evening, it appeared that none had. There was a bar down one side of a narrow room. There were tables on the other side. Beyond the narrow room there was a much wider one, with waiting, white-clothed tables. There was a man sitting on a stool behind the bar. He was reading the *New York Post*. He was wearing a dinner jacket—unexpected garb for a bartender.

"Opens at six," the man said, when Tony went up to the bar. "Got to give the staff a couple of hours off. Larry'll be along in a few minutes to open up."

Tony said he hadn't, at least primarily, come in for a drink. He said he wanted a couple of words with the headwaiter, or maitre d' or whatever. With whoever had been in charge at lunchtime.

"Go ahead," the man said. "I'm Ricardo. Headwaiter. What couple of words?"

Tony Cook identified himself. He showed his badge for verification.

"O.K., officer," Ricardo said, "what'll it be?" He turned to shelves of bottles behind the bar. Tony said it would be a dry manhattan, and watched Ricardo mix it. Ricardo used Jack Daniel's, a good deal to Tony's surprise. He twisted lemon peel over the drink. He held the twisted peel above the glass and raised his eyebrows at Tony Cook, who shook his head. Ricardo dropped the peel into a bin behind the bar.

"That the way Mr. Akins has his?" Tony said. Ricardo said, "Yeah," stepping a little out of character. Then he said, "What the hell, officer? What about Mr. Akins?"

"Regular customer?"

"Two or three times a week. Very fine gentleman, Mr. Akins is."

"He was in today? With his partner, Mr. Bradley?"

"Yes. What's this all about, officer?"

There was no reason not to tell him. It would be on

the six o'clock local news. It would be in the bulldog of the *Daily News*. A little later, it would be in the early edition of the *New York Times*.

"Mr. Bradley is dead," Tony said. "He fell out of his office window. We're trying to find out how it happened. Whether, could be, he was a little woozy."

"The kind of clientele we have, they don't get what you'd call woozy," Ricardo said. "If you mean intoxicated."

"All right," Tony said and sipped from his glass. The manhattan was good, although it was a bit excessive to add even the driest vermouth to Jack Daniel's. "Whatever word you want. Drunk. Falling-out-the-window drunk, Ricardo."

"No," Ricardo said. "Not any of the people who come here. High-class people. In advertising, most of them. Some editors and like that."

Tony's ignorance of people like that was not as complete as Nate Shapiro's—as Nate insisted it was, anyway. Rachel's acquaintance ranged rather widely. Now and then it overlapped Tony Cook. He had not found the advertising people, the painters, the occasional poet he had encountered with her especially noticeable for abstinence.

"We don't serve them if they look like having too much," Ricardo said. "Just sort of forget to serve an extra one, if you know what I mean. Not that we have to very often."

Tony was sure they didn't. "Mr. Akins comes in often," Tony said. "Probably signs for his lunches, I imagine."

"All right," Ricardo said. "All *right*. Soon as Larry shows up, I'll get out this noon's tabs. Drink all right, officer?"

"Fine," Tony said. "How much do I owe you?"

Ricardo looked at him and said, "Huh?" Tony didn't say anything. "O.K.," Ricardo said, "Two bucks." Tony gave him two dollar bills. A man came from the rear of Ad Lib. He wore a white jacket and dark trousers and a black bow tie. He joined Ricardo behind the bar, and Ricardo said, "O.K., Larry. All yours," and, to Tony Cook, "All right. If you'll just come along, officer."

Tony finished his drink and followed up two steps and into the dining area. The room was still empty of customers, but five waiters, all in dark green jackets and black bow ties, were sitting at a table in a far corner. They all stood up. Ricardo nodded his head at them, and they all sat down again. Ricardo led the way past a swinging door into a wide corridor and then to the right into a small room with its door open. There was a tall stool behind a counter, and Ricardo sat on it.

He reached down to a drawer beside the stool and took a pile of paper slips out of it. They were neatly lined together and there was a rubber band around them. The banded stack was thick. At least a hundred lunch checks, paid for or signed, Tony guessed. Ricardo went through them slowly, turning the ones inspected face down, in a neat pile. He was two thirds through the stack when he said, "Here we are, officer."

Somebody whose name was signed but indecipherable had served "br snap" and "ch sal" and five "bar," and Leslie Akins (just decipherably, if you knew what to expect), had signed the tab, which totaled $17.65. He had added, "T 2.50," which Tony thought was not especially generous of him.

Ricardo translated: one chef's salad. One broiled red snapper.

53

"The waiter?" Tony said. Ricardo looked again at the lunch check. He said, "André. You want, officer?" and Tony said, "Yes," and added that it would only take a minute or two.

They went back into the restaurant. The waiters had left the table. They were standing around the room, still empty of customers. Each had a folded white napkin over his left arm. Ricardo said, "André," and a tall, blond waiter said, "Yes, Mr. Ricardo," and came over to them.

"This gentleman is a police officer," Ricardo said. "He wants a word with you."

Ricardo had carried a sheaf of large menus out of the checking office. He straightened his already straight bow tie and went down into the bar area, the menus under his left arm. There were several men standing along the bar now, and there was a youngish couple at one of the small tables along the other side of the narrow room. Tony could almost see Ricardo's headwaiter smile through the back of Ricardo's head.

André said, "Sir?"

"You served Mr. Akins and Mr. Bradley at lunch today," Tony said. "That's right, isn't it?"

André said, "Sir," again, which Tony took to be an affirmative.

"You often wait on them?"

"On Mr. Akins, officer. The table he prefers is usually on my station. Mr. Bradley—oh, once a week, sir."

"They often have lunch together?"

"They're partners in a firm, I understand. Yes, they come in together now and then. Mr. Akins comes in more often. Sometimes brings friends with him."

"Today," Tony said, "was there anything different

about them? Different, I mean, from other times they had lunch together?"

André wasn't sure what he meant. "Different, sir?"

Tony Cook wasn't sure what he meant, either. He said, "Anything at all. In their attitudes toward each other, say?"

"Much as always," André said. "So far as I remember, anyway. I have four other tables on my station, sir. And we were short a bus this noon. Just didn't show up. Kids nowadays. Just two partners having lunch together. Mr. Bradley had a salad, sir, and Mr. Akins had the fish. Mr. Bradley usually has a chef's salad when he comes in, sir. Didn't eat all of it today. But he often doesn't."

"They had drinks before lunch, according to the check. Five drinks between them, apparently?"

"Certainly, sir. Mr. Akins had two dry manhattans, which is what he usually has. Mr. Bradley was drinking martinis today. Sometimes he has Tio Pepe. Or La Ina."

"But today martinis. Three of them, I take it. How large are the martinis, do you happen to know?"

"Ounce and a half, Larry makes them."

"Mr. Bradley specify the kind of gin, André?"

"Tanqueray."

Tony said, "Mmmm." He said, "Higher proof than most domestic gins, isn't it?"

"I believe so, officer."

"Three fairly stiff martinis and part of a salad," Tony said. "Anything very substantial in this chef's salad?"

"Strips of ham and chicken, sir. Sometimes anchovies and strips of cheese. Depends on the salad chef a little. It's always a large salad, sir."

"Yes," Tony said. "But today Mr. Bradley didn't

55

eat all of it, you say. Three stiffish drinks and a few strips of ham and cheese and chicken."

"And greens, sir."

"And greens, of course. Still not very substantial, would you say?"

André merely said, "Mmmm," which said nothing.

"And Mr. Bradley usually had sherry before lunch. He was all right when he went out today?"

"All right? Oh, of course, sir. I'm afraid I don't understand what this is—"

"After lunch," Tony said, "Mr. Bradley went back to his office and fell out a window. It killed him. We're trying to find out how it happened."

"That's very sad, sir. But Mr. Bradley was perfectly all right when he left the restaurant, sir."

Ricardo was leading the couple who had been at a table across from the bar up the two shallow steps into the dining area. He seated them at a table for two against the wall. He put drinks he had carried on a small tray in front of them. He laid big menus beside the drinks. Apparently they were not yet ready to order. Ricardo bowed and went back to the barroom. It was comfortably filled now. Tony had been wrong about Ad Lib's being only a lunch place. He said "Thank you" to Ricardo as he passed him on his way out of the restaurant. Ricardo said, "Sir."

Tony wasn't certain that thanks were due. Oh, for apparent cooperation, certainly. But not, just as surely, for clearing things up.

Frank Bradley had had a very light lunch and three stiffish drinks. He had been described as a slight man, and poundage was supposed to be related to susceptibility to alcohol. Only that didn't always work—that was theory. One reasonably heavy man Tony knew could get noticeably drunk on a single two-ounce drink of 86.5-proof whiskey.

Tony walked on toward the precinct station house.

* * * * *

Morton Street is deep in Greenwich Village, but the squad-car driver had no trouble finding it. The house, an ex-town house from the looks of it, stood across the street from a row of old law tenements. Shapiro went up four rather worn steps to the door of the four-story town house. He expected to find a small vestibule with the usual array of mailboxes and doorbells. He did not. He found a single button and pressed it. Maybe it wasn't an "ex"-town house. Maybe it was entirely Timothy Langhorn's house.

A bell sounded inside, but nothing else happened. Shapiro pushed the button again, and waited again. Then there was sound of movement inside and the door opened. The man who opened it was a short man with a neatly trimmed gray beard.

Shapiro said, "Mr. Langhorn?"

"Dr. Atwood. Langhorn's a tenant of mine. You want to see him?"

Nate Shapiro said he did, Doctor. "Of philosophy," the gray-bearded man said. "Just go on down. He's down there, for all I know. Stairs at the end of the hall."

Then he turned and went up a flight of stairs. He turned on a light at the head of the stairs he climbed. Shapiro went along the unlighted hallway and found a flight of stairs leading down. There was no door at the head of the stairs, but there was light at the bottom of them. Shapiro went down the stairs. There was no door at the bottom of them, either; nothing to knock on. Shapiro walked into a sizable room, furnished as a living

57

room. High in the wall opposite were two windows, both small and with iron bars beyond them. Through them, Shapiro could see the lower ends of legs—the legs, obviously, of people walking along Morton Street. Mr. Langhorn lived in a basement. There was no sign of Mr. Langhorn; there was no sign of anybody.

Shapiro said, "Hullo?" He did not speak loudly. When there was no response except a muted echo, he said it again, loudly this time. This time he got an answer. It was, "God damn it to hell." The male voice was a heavy one. It sounded angry.

A door beside the stairs opened, and the man who came out was a big man in, at a guess, his middle thirties. He had only moderately long yellow hair. He was built rather like a football player. He was wearing a pair of yellow shorts. He looked at Nathan Shapiro and was tall enough to look down at him, although Shapiro is not a short man—lean, but not short. He said, "Want something? If the professor's sent you to do something about the furnace, no soap."

"If you're Timothy Langhorn," Shapiro said, "I'd like a few words with you. About Mr. Frank Bradley."

"You his lawyer? Something like that? Mean to say the son of a bitch is going to start to make sense?"

"I'm a policeman," Shapiro said. "Mr. Bradley is dead. You are Mr. Langhorn?"

The big man said, "Dead? The bastard's dead? Yes, I'm Langhorn. He was all right this afternoon. Wily as ever. Crooked as ever, come to that."

"That was before he fell out of his office window, Mr. Langhorn. A few minutes, apparently, after you were in his office. After you told him he'd sure as hell find out. Find out what, Mr. Langhorn?"

"That any of your business, Mr. Policeman?"

"Shapiro. Detective lieutenant. Homicide Squad. Yes, it may be, Mr. Langhorn. Since his secretary didn't hear him answer when you called back to him as you were closing the door."

"Look," Langhorn said, and now the anger seemed to have seeped out of his voice, "you say he fell out the window. And you say you're a Homicide dick. You figure somebody pushed him, is that it?"

"We're investigating that possibility, Mr. Langhorn. When you were in his office, did you feel that he was—well, depressed? Or that, perhaps, he'd been drinking?"

"Bradley was a guy you couldn't depress with a pile driver," Langhorn said. "If you mean was he drunk, I didn't notice it. I just said my piece and about all he did was to look tolerant and shake his head. I couldn't tell if he was even listening. Of course, he was sitting down. At his desk. Sometimes, people sit sober and walk drunk, if you know what I mean. Speaking of drinks?"

Shapiro shook his head.

"Not on duty, huh? Or is it not with a suspect?"

"I just don't want a drink, Mr. Langhorn."

"Well," Langhorn said, "I do, if that's all right with you, Lieutenant. You did say 'lieutenant,' didn't you?"

He did not wait to be answered. He walked across the room and opened one of the two doors side by side to the left of the high, barred windows. He went into a small kitchen, barely big enough to hold him. Shapiro heard ice cubes clatter out of a tray into a container. He heard the soft gurgle of liquid from a bottle. Langhorn came out and closed the kitchen door behind him. The kitchen was, obviously, under the Morton Street sidewalk. On the sidewalk, a small boy in a T-shirt crouched down and looked in one of the windows.

Langhorn said, "Scram, brat!" loudly. Another small boy appeared outside the other window. Langhorn put a short glass down on a table and sat on a sofa beyond the table. He shook his fist at the peering boys, and both of the boys laughed.

"Damn kids," Langhorn said, with no animus in his voice. "Probably think I'm something in a zoo cage. No privacy, but the professor lets me have it cheap. Barges down himself, in the winter, to diddle with the furnace. Never does it any good, of course. About what you'd expect from a professor of philosophy, I suppose. May as well sit down and get on with it, Lieutenant. For your information, I didn't push the son of a bitch out the window. And I wouldn't blame anybody who did. O.K. with you?"

Shapiro sat down on the other side of the table from the big man in shorts. He said, "I take it you didn't like Mr. Bradley?"

"Don't make much of a secret of it, do I? For my money, he was a slippery son of a bitch. That partner of his is too, I guess. And it *is* my money, damn it. Get what I mean?"

"No, Mr. Langhorn," Shapiro said. "I'm afraid I don't. You say you said your piece to Bradley this afternoon. What was your piece, Mr. Langhorn?"

"That he'd gypped me," Langhorn said. "Know anything about performance rights, Lieutenant? TV rights, for instance?"

Shapiro was afraid he didn't.

Langhorn drank deeply from his glass. He put it down on the table. "Few years ago, I guess I didn't, either. What my lawyer says, anyway. Went to him too late, or damn near too late, he says. After the horse was stolen. Maybe he can get the horse back, he thinks. Maybe not.

Only part of the horse, at best. Lawyers cost a hell of a lot of money, you know."

Shapiro agreed that lawyers could be expensive. He said, "You're not really making things a lot clearer, Mr. Langhorn. Why did you dislike Mr. Bradley so much?"

"Looking for motive, aren't you? Only, the catch is, I didn't throw him out of the window. That's your catch, I mean. Aren't you supposed to tell me about my constitutional rights, Lieutenant?"

"I'm not charging you with anything. Just trying to get understandable answers to some questions. Answers I can understand. You're not helping much, are you?"

Unexpectedly, Langhorn laughed. Then he said, "Maybe I'm not, at that. I worked all this morning, all this afternoon after I got back from seeing Bradley. Leaves me a little fuzzy, I guess. And then you barge in and throw this at me. Also, trying to get some sense out of Bradley always—well, gets me sore. At the whole damn world."

There didn't seem to be much to say to that, so Shapiro didn't say anything. He merely waited, letting the expression on his long, sad face make it clear he was waiting.

"O.K.," Langhorn said. "I'll spell it out for you. I'm a writer; a professional writer. I make my living writing. Such as my living is. I used to write fiction, when they were still buying fiction. Made-up stories, if you know what I mean?"

He paused, as if for an answer.

Trying to ride me, Nate Shapiro thought. "I have a normal vocabulary, Mr. Langhorn," he said. "You used to write fiction. Now you write what? Articles? Essays? Political commentaries?"

"Whatever I can sell, it comes down to. Sometimes

I get assignments. Sometimes I just write pieces and my agent—oh, makes paper airplanes out of them and shoots them out the window. To fall to earth he knows not where. All right, sometimes he sells them and I can pay the rent on my cage in the zoo. Keeps the professor happy. Decent old guy, the professor. If he'd only leave that damn furnace alone." He took another swallow from his glass. "Seems to me I'm wandering," he said. "Bradley doesn't seem to come into it, does he, Shapiro?"

"No."

"Six-seven years ago I wrote a detective story. Mystery novel. Whatever you want to call it. What I called it was *Brook No Evil*. Seemed like a good title at the time. About a young married couple named Brook, who ran a private detective agency. Solved murders. That sort of thing. I don't suppose you read mysteries very much, Lieutenant? Or think much of private eyes?"

"I've read some, Mr. Langhorn. Private investigators get divorce evidence, for the most part. I didn't, I'm afraid, read this one of yours."

"Three of them, actually. *Brook No Evil, Brink of Death, The Glass Knife*. All about Paul and Enid Brook. Did all right, as such things do. You know what, Lieutenant, people get the idea if you have a book published, you make a fortune. People, for God's sake! Oh, sometimes. You know what Eisenhower made out of that book of his, years ago?"

Shapiro shook his head.

"Neither do I," Langhorn said. "But it was all capital gains. Because, believe it or not, he wasn't a professional writer. You invent a gadget, and that's capital gains. You invent characters and things that happen to them, and is what you get in royalties capital gains? Hell, no. That's just something for the Internal Revenue Service to eat whole. You donate your vice-presidential papers to—"

"All right, Mr. Langhorn. It isn't a fair world. That's already been pointed out. These mystery novels you wrote. They have something to do with Bradley?"

Shapiro was damn right they did.

"Around three years ago, Bradley got in touch with me. He had his own advertising agency then. Before he hooked up with Akins. He said he thought the Brook couple might go as a TV series, and that he'd like to get an option on the rights. Offered a thousand dollars for a three-year option to make a pilot to show the networks and sponsors. Three years, for God's sake. I didn't have an agent then. Thought I'd be throwing away the ten percent. All right, I was a damn fool. And I could use the thousand."

"So you gave Mr. Bradley the option?"

"For a thousand dollars. A *three-year* option. The agent I've got now says he probably could have got me a thousand a year, and maybe five if they made a pilot. And that only a damn fool would have let Bradley slip that clause in."

Shapiro raised his eyebrows.

"O.K. Listen to this, Lieutenant. 'The option rights herein granted by the author shall remain in effect for three years from the date of this agreement and then, providing no sale as described above has been completed, terminate, further providing, however, that if bona fide negotiations for such a sale are in progress at the time this option would otherwise terminate, this agreement shall remain in effect until such a time as such negotiations are concluded, and the author further agrees that Bradley shall be the sole judge as to whether such conclusion has been reached.' Gobbledygook, isn't it? My agent says he never saw anything like it and my lawyer says maybe it's defective. 'Flagrantly inequitable,' he says and that we can sue to break the agreement. He thinks we'd have a good chance of winning. If we don't, you see where it leaves—left—Bradley, don't you?"

"Yes. He could have said at any time that he was negotiating a sale. When does this option expire?"

"The first of September."

"When Mr. Bradley joined Mr. Akins in this new firm, he assigned his option to the firm, I suppose?"

"What he told me."

"And that he, or the firm, is negotiating to sell the rights? Or to make this pilot film?"

"What he told me today."

"If such a film is made, with this Brook couple in it, you get a further payment, I suppose?"

"Just a flat payment. Five thousand, and then Folsom, Akins and Bradley, or whatever it turns out to be with Bradley dead, have the rights forever. What they call 'in perpetuity.' My agent says he never heard of such a lousy deal and that I must have been nuts. And now with this other deal coming up—what time is it, Lieutenant?"

Shapiro told the big man in pale yellow shorts that it was six thirty-five. Langhorn said, "Jesus Christ. I've got to get some clothes on. I've got somebody coming at seven."

"If you'll just—" Shapiro said, and stopped because he was talking to a rapidly receding back. Langhorn moved very fast for such a big man. There was no point in talking to the closed door of what was evidently Langhorn's bedroom.

Shapiro lighted a cigarette, wondered whether he was ever going to get home to Brooklyn, and a shower and, most of all, Rose, and looked around the room. Only the street side was really basement, he realized. At the back, french doors opened on a wooden-fenced garden. There was even grass growing in the garden, and beyond the doors were two open deck chairs turned toward a table between them. There was even a faint breeze stirring the canvas of the deck chairs. Shapiro went out through the doorway. It wasn't really any cooler outside, but there was a listless movement of air. He sat in one of the chairs and smoked his cigarette.

There was a wall on his left as he sat facing the garden—back yard, more accurately. It would, he thought, be the wall of the rest of Langhorn's apartment. There was a small, partly open window in the wall. The sound of splashing water came through the window. Langhorn was having a shower. Nathan Shapiro looked again at his watch. Langhorn had fifteen minutes to get his clothes on before his "somebody" was due. Shapiro mildly wished he had accepted the offer of a drink. Except that if Langhorn had sherry at all, it would probably be what they called "dry." Unpleasant, acid-tasting stuff.

The sound of splashing water stopped. Shapiro went inside and sat where he had sat before. He regarded Langhorn's emptied glass. He wondered about this "other deal." He wondered why Bill Weigand always sent him to grope through alien land. If he were still a uniformed cop walking a Brooklyn beat, he would be home by now. If, of course, he had the eight-to-four shift. Well, it was his own fault that he was in the Detective Division, New York Police Department. That he had asked for. It had been the department's absurd decision to make him a lieutenant. He had taken the examination just to see how he'd make out. He had placed undue reliance on departmental judgment.

Langhorn started to whistle on the far side of his bedroom door. It was cheerful whistling. Was Langhorn cheerful because he had successfully pushed a man out a window? Langhorn was certainly big enough to do that, if he wanted to. But, if Langhorn was telling the truth about this option business, where would killing Frank Bradley have got him?

There was, of course, no special reason to assume that Langhorn was telling the truth. Or that anybody he and Tony Cook had talked to was.

5

A PRELIMINARY REPORT from the Medical Examiner's office had reached precinct by the time Tony Cook got there. The cadaver was that of a male Caucasian, approximately five feet nine inches tall and weighing one hundred and thirty pounds, again approximately. Death had resulted from multiple injuries, consistent with those resulting from a fall of seventy feet or so and a landing on a hard surface. "What they mean is, he was all smashed up," precinct-squad Detective Thomas Fuller told Tony, rather needlessly. Fuller, on the four-to-midnight shift, had got the report out of files for Tony. Further tests were not yet completed.

Captain Fremont and Detective Kenneth Latham were off duty. The four-to-midnight had taken over. It had not as yet been able to get in touch with Mrs. Bradley. A man from the Suffolk County, Long Island, police had checked. He had found only a maid and had been told that Mrs. Bradley was not at home; that she had gone to New York and might stay there overnight. A telephone call to a Manhattan number had got no answer.

"Let's try it again," Tony Cook said.

Fuller tried again the number of the Bradleys' New York apartment. After two rings he got "The Bradley residence." Yes, Mrs. Bradley had just got in. This was Timkins speaking. Who should he tell Mrs. Bradley was calling?

There are certain things the New York City police prefer not to handle by telephone. Fuller gave his name to the man who said he was Timkins and said he had a matter to take up with Mrs. Bradley and that he'd be along if Timkins would just tell Mrs. Bradley he was coming and ask her not to go out until he got there. "You say *Detective* Fuller?"

"That's right," Fuller said, and hung up. Tony said he guessed he'd ride along, if that would be all right. As detective first grade to detective third grade it was all right and they went in a squad car to an address in the lower East Fifties. The apartment building was tall and new, and the Bradleys had a penthouse. A woman opened the door for them. She was a small, trim woman. She was deeply tanned; the sun had etched tiny wrinkles on her face. To Tony, she looked to be in her middle thirties. Yes, she was Mrs. Bradley.

Tony left it to Fuller. After all, it had happened in Fuller's precinct.

"I'm afraid there's been an accident, Mrs. Bradley," Fuller said. "To your husband, I'm afraid. A—a very bad accident, I'm afraid."

For several seconds she merely stood and looked at them. But her weathered face set, as if it had suddenly frozen. Certainty had frozen it, Tony thought. Her lips seemed too frozen for speech. But after a time they managed words. Her voice was brittle, a frozen voice.

"Frank's dead," she said. "That's what you're trying to tell me, isn't it?"

Fuller said he was afraid so.

"When Timkins said it was a detective, I knew it would be—would be something like that," she said. "You may as well come on in, I suppose." She turned and walked away from them into a large living room. One side of the room was almost completely glass, and Manhattan Island was jagged beyond the glass. A few lights were coming on in the city's buildings.

The room was rectangular, and the glass was on the far long side. She walked down the room to a bar at the end of the room, and tapped a bell. The ringing of the bell was unexpectedly loud. A man wearing a white jacket came through a door behind the bar and said, "Yes, Mrs. Bradley?"

"Make me a drink, Timkins," she said. "These gentlemen too, if they'd like."

Timkins said, "Certainly, madam. Bourbon?"

"Yes," she said. "Stiff." And her voice was stiff. "I don't know about the gentlemen. They've brought bad news, Timkins. Very bad news. About Mr. Bradley."

He said, "I'm sorry, Mrs. Bradley," but she did not appear to hear him. She walked back up the room and sat in a chair, her back to Manhattan. Timkins, who was a small, white-faced man, said, "Gentlemen?" Fuller and Tony Cook shook their heads, and Timkins went behind the small bar. He used tongs to put ice cubes in a medium-sized glass. He poured a good deal of whiskey on the cubes. He carried her drink to Mrs. Bradley on a small silver tray, and she said, "Thank you, Timkins. That will be all for now, I think." He said, "Madam," and went back through the door behind the bar.

Tony and Detective Fuller went over and stood in

front of the small woman, who was wearing a short, dark-blue dress. It had a high collar, tight around her slender neck.

"Timkins said 'Fuller,'" she said. "One of you is named Fuller? Detective Fuller?"

They named themselves for her.

"Sit down," she said. "Tell me what happened."

Fuller looked at Tony Cook.

"Your husband fell out of his office window, Mrs. Bradley," Tony Cook said. "He was alone in the office at the time. He—well, he must have died instantly. We don't know how he happened to fall. The window was wide open when his secretary went in. To see why he didn't answer when she spoke to him on the intercom. To say that you were on the phone. You did call him, Mrs. Bradley? At a little after three this afternoon?"

"Yes. To tell him I was in town. That I thought I'd stay in the apartment overnight. And the girl who answered said something like 'Just a moment, Mrs. Bradley.' Then I heard her say, 'Mr. Bradley, your wife is on the phone.' Something like that. Then she said that apparently he'd stepped out of his office and that if I'd wait, she'd try to find him. And then—then nothing. Nothing at all. You mean—mean that it was while I was waiting on the phone that Frank—that he was—"

For the first time, there was shakiness in her brittle voice.

"A few minutes before that, probably," Tony said.

"I just waited and waited," she said. "I think I said 'Hullo?' once or twice. The way one does, you know. But nobody answered, so finally I hung up. And called here. Told Timkins I was going to be here tonight. So that he would have things ready. To—well, warn him, I suppose you'd call it."

70

"I see," Tony Cook said. "I gather you don't live here, Mrs. Bradley? In this apartment, I mean."

"Not in the summers," she said. "I can't stand the city in the summer. And Frank won't have the air conditioning on. He has—had—a thing about it. So I stay out at our place on the Island. And Frank usually came out for weekends. Unless he was tied up in town, as he was sometimes."

"This past weekend," Tony said. "Did Mr. Bradley get out to Long Island?"

"I don't see what that has to do with anything. But no, he didn't. He called Friday and told me he couldn't make it. That he looked like being tied up all day Saturday. And it's a long trip for just one day in the country, you know. Way out on the Island, our place is. Of course, we've always come into town after the holidays and stay until the middle of March. The eastern end of the Island can get—well, rather rugged in January and February, you know."

Tony said, "Yes," indicating he did know. Which was not especially true. He had spent years avoiding Long Island.

"You came into town today, Mrs. Bradley," Tony said. "Any particular reason?"

"To see my—no, I don't see that that's any business of yours, Mr.—what did you say your name is?"

"Cook. Detective Anthony Cook, Homicide Squad. No, probably it isn't, Mrs. Bradley. We just try to get the whole picture."

Something like a smile moved on her lips.

"I didn't, Detective Cook, come into town to push my husband out a window. Apparently, you think somebody did push him. You did say 'Homicide,' you know."

"We're just trying to eliminate that possibility,"

Tony said. "As a matter of routine. You were on the telephone a few minutes after your husband fell. Not that we have any reason to suspect you of anything, Mrs. Bradley. Do you mind telling me where you were when you made the phone call? Trying to reach your husband to tell him you planned to stay in town overnight?"

"In—in a friend's office. Way downtown. And—I can prove it, Detective Cook."

There was animosity in her voice, now. Not grief. There hadn't really been grief at any time, Tony thought. Shock, certainly. But people show grief in many different ways. Tony had brought bad news often enough to learn that.

He told Mrs. Bradley—no first name as yet, but precinct would have that—that she would be notified when her husband's body was available for burial. Or, if she preferred, the notification could go through her husband's lawyers. He'd need the name of the lawyers in any case. That was part of the routine they had to go through.

She gave him names—four of them, Kornfeld, Yarborough, Vincent and Goldstein—and a Wall Street address. Tony told her how sorry they both were to have brought her such bad news. She merely nodded her head to that, and finished what remained of her stiff drink.

The squad car took Tony down to 230 East Twenty-first Street, where everything was modern, and even air-conditioned, and which was a damn long way from Tony's apartment in West Twelfth. Life had been simpler when Homicide, Manhattan South, had had its squad room in the West Twenties, within walking distance of West Twelfth. Which, in turn, was an easy walk from Gay Street.

Tony went up to the second-floor squad room. Detective Lieutenant Nathan Shapiro wasn't there. He hadn't checked in. Tony Cook sat down to wait. It was almost seven-thirty. It was one hell of an eight-to-four. Of course, it often was. It was also, often a hell of a four-to-midnight. Or a midnight-to-eight, come to that.

* * * * *

It was not quite seven o'clock when Timothy Langhorn came back into his living room. He had made good time, Nathan Shapiro thought. He had also made quite a change.

Langhorn was wearing a dark-blue summer suit. It fitted beautifully on his big frame. It even, for some reason, made him look bigger than he had before. The material of the jacket was a little pebbled. There were tiny knots in it. Nathan recognized the material because of the tiny irregularities. Rose had tried to get him to get a suit of that material. She had said she was tired of his tired gray suits—of both of them. She had said he would look fine in a suit made of Italian silk, and that the little knots in the fabric were something the silk-worms did. Nathan had said he wasn't up to a suit made of Italian silk, and they had compromised on another gray suit. It wasn't too tired, yet.

Langhorn was definitely up to a blue summer suit of Italian silk. He was up to a paler blue shirt and a bow tie of darker blue. Also, he had shaved again. This somebody, due now in about five minutes, must be a special somebody.

"This new deal coming up, Mr. Langhorn," Shapiro said. "Want to tell me about it?"

"Sure you won't have a drink?" Langhorn said.

Shapiro shook his head. He said, "Thanks, anyway," matching the new amiability in the big man's voice. "About this deal?"

Langhorn sat down across the coffee table from Nathan Shapiro.

"No reason why not," Langhorn said. "Just a ghost of a deal, probably, unless this guy Akins will make more sense than Bradley would. Goddamn dog in the manger, Bradley was. Akins probably will be too. Probably runs in the firm. And these new people want an answer, Fred says."

What was that line Rose quoted sometimes? About cats. Of course. "Make their point by walking around it." By somebody named Graves.

"Fred's my agent," Langhorn said. "He's been dickering with some West Coast outfit. Thinks they're ready to come through if we can shake off the manger dogs. Good outfit, Fred says it is. He's dealt with them before. Only, they want an answer. Like as of yesterday. As I told that son of a bitch Bradley this afternoon. Dead son of a bitch now, you say."

"Yes, Mr. Langhorn. Mr. Bradley is dead. This West Coast outfit?"

"Independent producers. Also after the Brook characters. Think it's time for a soft-sell series, Fred says. Think people are getting fed with private eyes who spend most of their time smashing up cars and taking shots at each other. It's always the villains who miss. Ever noticed that, Lieutenant?"

"I don't watch TV much," Shapiro said. "You are talking about TV, I take it?"

"Sure. Want to know what this outfit is ready to come up with?"

Shapiro did want to know.

"A thousand on signature for a three-month option. With no phony escape clause. Five thousand if they make a pilot. And—listen to this, Lieutenant. If they sell it as a series, five hundred for each thirty-minute show.

Seven fifty for ninety minutes. A thousand for a two-hour special. Every week, that could be. To me, less Fred's ten. Sign tomorrow if the dogs will get out of the manger. And, that's just for the rights, Shapiro. I just sit back and collect."

"The—stories? I mean, the plots for the—episodes? The dialogue? You don't have to—"

"The scripts, you mean. Hell, no. Get those from members of the Screen Writers Guild. At so much a script. Nothing to do with me. I get paid for the rights, period. I—" He stopped suddenly. He lighted a cigarette and regarded Shapiro across the coffee table. The blue of his shirt matched, Shapiro noticed, the blue of his eyes.

"I'm giving myself a hell of a good motive, aren't I?" Langhorn said. "And you sit there lapping it up. Thirty-nine weeks at five hundred a week. Maybe seven fifty. And half that for each summer rerun, if it really took hold. Of course, maybe only thirteen. You can't ever tell."

"It does involve a good deal of money," Shapiro said.

"Just for signing my name," Langhorn said. "And sitting on my ass. And, you're thinking, pushing a skinny guy out a window."

"I'm not thinking anything—yet," Shapiro said.

"There's always this guy Akins, Lieutenant. Ready to louse it up. I saw him once when I was up there. He's not so skinny."

Shapiro said he hadn't forgotten Mr. Akins. And, from the head of the stairs, somebody said, "Anybody home?" The voice was soft. There was a croon in it, but it carried clearly down the stairs. It was very female. So was the click of heels on the stair treads, as Langhorn's "somebody" came down them. Langhorn stood up. So did Nathan Shapiro. Langhorn said, "Hi," and there was sudden lightness in his previously heavy voice.

"And about time, too," he added to the slim, very pretty girl who came into the room. She had come fast down the stairs, Nathan thought. She had hurried down the stairs.

She stopped at the foot of the stairs and looked at Shapiro, who thought he was too obviously in the way. Of course, policemen often are.

"Thought I'd never get a cab," the girl said.

There was a suggestion of red in her blond hair. Her face was small, delicate. But there was a marked decisiveness in her features. She had a noticeably visible face, in spite of the delicacy of nose and lips. She had a high, almost straight-up-and-down forehead. Shapiro felt, vaguely, that he was somehow familiar with her face. She wore a short summer dress, with squares and oblongs and, yes, crescents, of black on a white background. She carried a wisp of a white sweater over her left arm.

Langhorn was across the room in two long strides. He put his arms around the girl. From where Shapiro sat, the big man seemed to engulf her. She did not seem to mind.

After a few seconds, Langhorn put a hand on each of her shoulders and held her away from him. "After a trip like that, I'd be bushed," Langhorn said. "Utterly and completely. And here you look fresh as a—" He hesitated.

"The word is 'daisy,' " the girl said. "Or bright as a button. But you won't ever use just the words other people use, will you?"

"Fresh as a sunrise," Langhorn said. "Not if I can think of another, pet. Peg of my heart."

She looked up at him and made a grimace. It was

very expressive. I needn't have worried about being in the way, Shapiro thought. They don't know I'm here. Maybe I ought to cough. Or clear my throat or something.

But then Langhorn turned to face Shapiro. He kept an arm around the girl's shoulders, so that both of them faced him.

"We have company, Peg," Langhorn said. "Lieutenant Shapiro. He's a cop kind of lieutenant, Peg. And he's here on business. Miss Peggy Claymore, Lieutenant."

There was something in his tone which made Shapiro feel he was expected to say, "Not *the* Peggy Claymore?" He found he had no such inclination. He merely said, "Miss Claymore."

"Business," the girl said. "With you, Tim? You been up to something, darling? Not that I'd put it past you. Involving some poor innocent female, I shouldn't wonder."

"No," Langhorn said. "I don't involve innocent females." There was still a trace of laughter under his voice. But that disappeared when he went on. "He thinks maybe I'm a murderer, Peggy. Thinks maybe I pushed a man out of a window. I didn't, but that's what he thinks. Right, Lieutenant?"

"We don't know that anybody pushed," Shapiro said. "Just think it's possible. I've just been asking Mr. Langhorn a few questions, Miss Claymore. Not accusing him of anything."

"Because," Langhorn said, "the man who went out the window was named Bradley. And I'd been at his office just before he—"

Peggy Claymore's eyes widened and the muscles tightened around her lips.

"Not *Frank* Bradley," she said. "Not *that* Bradley." Her soft voice went up.

Langhorn looked down at her. There was, Shapiro thought, surprise in his face. Even, perhaps, astonishment. He did not say anything. He merely waited. She looked up at him.

"All the way across the country," she said. "In that damn airplane. I was supposed to see him tomorrow morning. He wired me to come. About a part. The part of Enid, Tim."

"My Enid?" Langhorn said.

She nodded her head. She said, "Your Enid, Tim. Enid Brook. You mean—mean you didn't know?"

He shook his head.

"No," he said. "He said he was just negotiating. I *thought* the son of a bitch was lying. Stalling me off. You mean he was already casting?"

"What he said in the telegram. Bert Owen to play Paul. Me Enid. I don't know who else. He's got a producer, apparently. But he was going to direct."

"A script?"

"It sounded like it, Tim. All ready to go, it sounded like. So I wired you I was coming and got on that damn plane. God, how I hate airplanes! And Ralph just about had me lined up for something. Just a bit, but something. He's sore as hell, incidentally."

Langhorn tightened Peggy Claymore against him. But he spoke to Nathan Shapiro. He said, "You getting this, Lieutenant?"

"Most of it, I think," Shapiro said. "Miss Claymore is an actress. Bradley was going to make a movie based on this book of yours. For television. Was going to offer Miss Claymore the part of Enid—Enid Brook, you said, didn't you? A private detective. And he was about ready to start—start shooting."

"The way it looks," Langhorn said. "Behind my back, while the option holds. And all the time I thought he was just stalling me off." He paused for a moment. "I'll be damned," he said. "The tricky son of a bitch. And all you said in your wire, Peg, was that you thought you'd make it by around seven."

"I supposed you knew," Peggy said. "I supposed of course you knew, dear."

"The author," Timothy Langhorn said, "is always the last one to know." He added, "I'll be damned," but his voice was muted. He appeared to consider the matter further. "The son of a bitch," he said. His tone was conversational.

"He had an option," Peggy Claymore said. "You told me that. He just decided to exercise it. And, Tim, I supposed you knew all about it. I really did. I—you ought to know I wouldn't go behind your back."

"Darling," Langhorn said, "it's not anything you did. I'd love to have you play Enid. You'd be perfect for it. It was Bradley who went behind my back, probably with a knife in his hand. It was—" He did not finish. He merely drew Peggy closer against him.

"Apparently Miss Claymore is right," Shapiro said. "Mr. Bradley merely exercised his option, which, you say, had until September first to run."

"He'd have owed me five thousand," Timothy Langhorn said. "And this afternoon he was 'just negotiating.' What he told me. So now what?"

"I don't know," Shapiro said. "My guess would be the firm takes over and probably goes ahead with it. Bradley did assign the option to the firm when he joined it? Became Mr. Akins's partner?"

"What he told me."

"So if Akins makes this what you call a pilot he'll have to pay you the five thousand?"

"Chicken feed, Lieutenant."

Langhorn, Nathan thought, knew rather pampered chickens. He also thought that seven-thirty was a late hour to call Rose and tell her he wouldn't be home at four-thirty. And that Langhorn's option—Leslie Akins's option now, apparently—probably had nothing to do with Frank Bradley's fall from a window. He told Timothy Langhorn that he'd probably be in touch, and the pretty girl with the actor's face that it was pleasant to have met her.

He climbed the stairs from Langhorn's basement—half basement, actually—and let himself out of Professor Atwood's house. He rather doubted that Langhorn and Peggy Claymore noticed he had gone. A most handsome couple they made, Nathan thought. Not the sort of people he'd ever understand, of course.

He had the car stop at the first telephone booth they came to. Rose answered on the first ring. So, more loudly, did Cleo, their little Scottie bitch. Cleo always assumes that any telephone ringing means a call for her.

"Yes, dear," Rose Shapiro said. "I'd gathered as much. The roast will be overdone, I'm afraid. But it's used to that. And I know you do and that you're sorry. And I do you and it was my idea to marry a policeman. I'll take the roast out. About an hour, you think? . . . Oh, just cramming, as usual."

Rose was cramming for her doctorate. Within six months or so, she would go up for her orals. Then, Nathan was quite certain, he would be married to Dr. Rose Shapiro and, presumably, to the principal of Clayton High School, instead, as now, to the assistant principal. He would remain a detective lieutenant unless the department came to its senses and moved him back to detective, first grade.

Tony Cook was waiting at his desk in East Twenty-first Street. They filled each other in.

"Bradley offered Rachel a part in this Brook film," Tony said. "The part of the girl who gets murdered, she says. I meant to tell you. But it sort of got joggled out of my mind. She and I saw this Claymore girl in a play a while back. Good, we both thought, and damn pretty. If you like the type."

Shapiro agreed that Miss Peggy Claymore was a very pretty girl and that it had been a good idea of Tony's to ask the Suffolk County police for any background they had on Mr. and Mrs. Frank Bradley. And that it might be another good idea to check on the law firm of Kornfeld, Yarborough, Vincent and Goldstein and ask whether Mrs. Bradley had made a telephone call from their offices at a little after three o'clock on the afternoon of Monday, July fifteenth. And also, if she was in the offices, if she was there to consult a member, or associate, of the firm. And if so, what about.

"Not that they'll tell us, probably," Tony said.

Nathan agreed they probably wouldn't and went home to Brooklyn.

6

EIGHT-THIRTY IN THE MORNING would not be an hour at which Rachel Farmer would welcome a telephone call. If she had an early job, which sometimes she had, she would be dressing to go to it. If she didn't have, she would be asleep. She would have to bear with him, Tony thought. Probably she would. It was a small loose end. A corroboration, if anything at all. But he might as well tie it up—and hope she wouldn't be angry. He got an outside line and dialed a familiar number. Her phone rang four times before she answered it. She said, "Tony! What an hour!" But that, no, she hadn't been asleep.

"This guy likes to paint in the mornings," she said. "Something about the light. But when he gets done, you'd think he'd painted in the dark. I was looking at the 'Today' show and—oh, my God. Hold on a minute, Tony."

He held on.

"—poaching an egg," Rachel said. "Now it's as hard

as a rock. I hate them hard. Is it about poor Mr. Bradley? It has to be about something or you wouldn't call at this unearthly hour."

"Yes," Tony said, "it's about Bradley."

"It was on the local news part," she said. "Just a snippet. I gather he was pushed. And that I'm still not going to be an actress. But I didn't think you'd listened to a word I said."

Tony told her he always listened to her—unless distracted. He said, "Bradley offered you this part. In a pilot film for TV. When was that, dear?"

"Friday afternoon. Up at this what they call a studio. A barn of a place. Apparently used to be a real movie studio. Way up on Broadway. I was a typical housewife in a perfectly awful outfit, rubbing something on a wall, and saying I always used it to bring out the hidden luster in the wood, which it penetrates deeply. It's a thirty-second spot, and I'm on about fifteen. It took three hours to get it the way he wanted it."

"Well," Tony said, "you get paid by the hour. To get it the way Bradley wanted it?"

"The photographer. Do you suppose anything really penetrates wood, Tony? The scalp, maybe, like this thing I did a while back. 'Lusterglow. Restores youth's luster to your hair.' I was glamorous in that one. Wearing as little as TV allows. But *wood*, Tony? Even with lemon in it. Of course, everything has lemon in it nowadays. Lemon is *in*, Tony."

"Bradley?"

"All right. I'm scatterbrained in the morning. He was there. Sort of—oh, supervising. Making suggestions. 'Try the other profile this time.' That sort of thing. When they finally got through and I'd changed and got the makeup off, he was waiting for me. Everybody else had gone. It was about five, then, and he said I'd been very patient and maybe I could do with a drink. He also said that I'd been very good and that there was something he'd like to take up with me and that the Carlyle wasn't too far away and that their lounge was very good, and would be quiet that time of day. So we went, and I had Tio Pepe."

"Yes," Tony said. "And he had a very dry martini, made with Tanqueray?"

"Yes, I think so. A martini, anyway. Does it matter?"

Tony said it didn't matter. "And then?"

"He said they were doing a pilot for a possible television series and that there was a part he thought I'd be right for. A small part, he said. But this is what I told you already, Tony. I was to get murdered early on, but then there'd be these flashbacks, showing me while I'm still alive."

"You gathered he had the script ready?"

"He sounded like it. He talked about a read-through next week. If he could get this Peggy Claymore back from the Coast. And somebody named Owen to play the man. I said I'd love to try it, and he got me a cab and I went home."

"There were just the two of you, Rachel? Nobody else from the agency?"

"Just the two of us, yes. And there was almost nobody else in the lounge. Too early, I suppose."

"Did you at all get the feeling that the making of this pilot was in any way—well, hush-hush? Secret?"

"No. Why on earth should it be, Tony? And, Tony, I've really got to—"

"Yes," Tony said. "At any of the parties you go to down in the Village, did you ever run into a man named Langhorn? Timothy Langhorn. He's a writer. Big man, I understand. Big physically."

"Not that I remember offhand. Tony, I've got to get dressed and go. This guy is going to be cranky if I'm late. He's always cranky anyway. I don't think he sells very many of them."

"Go along," Tony said. Then he said, "Tonight, darling? Assuming I don't get stuck?"

"Fine," Rachel said. "About seven, if you don't get stuck."

* * * * *

Nathan Shapiro checked by telephone at a few minutes after nine. Mr. Akins usually reached his office about ten. Yes, when he got in he would be told that the lieutenant would like a few words with him. His secretary would know what his morning schedule was. His secretary was not in yet. Certainly Lieutenant Shapiro's message would be delivered when she got in. It *was* Shapiro? "Oh, thank *you,* sir."

Nathan brushed Cleo's forepaws off his knee and told her she didn't have to assist in making calls. It was enough for her to answer the telephone. She quit barking. She went away and came back with the leash in her mouth. Nathan told her she had already been for her walk and that she had been a good dog. She barked briefly in acknowledgment and dropped her leash for somebody to put away. Nathan strapped his gun on and put his suit jacket over it.

Rose was lying on her bed, with books scattered around her. She was reading Trollope. She was cramming and she said, "All right, dear," in answer to Nathan's report that he was going along. She looked up from the book and said, "Your other suit *is* back from the cleaner's, Nathan." Nathan said that tomorrow he'd remember and that he'd try to get back at a reasonable hour.

"You always try, darling," Rose said. "I will say that."

She put her book down and Shapiro leaned over and kissed her. She put her arms around him and said, "Be careful, Nathan," which she always said when he left in the morning.

Cleo tried to get out the door with him and was rebuffed. She barked a protest. Rose said, "Come here, dog," and Cleo went there. All was in order at the Shapiros'. Routine held.

It was after nine, so the subway wasn't quite as jammed as usual. There were no seats, of course. Nathan held onto a strap to the Twenty-third Street stop. Tony Cook was at his desk in the squad room. He was talking on the telephone. He raised his free hand as Shapiro came into the room. Shapiro digressed from his way to his own office and went to Cook's desk. Cook said, "Thank you, Captain," and cradled the telephone.

"Suffolk County people," Tony said. "Full of co-operation. Bradleys are well known out there. Very high-class people, apparently. She's Sylvia Towne Bradley. Towne with an *e*. She's women's golf champion at the Towne Country Club. Her grandfather founded it. But it was her great-grandfather who built the house. The 'mansion,' the captain called it. Captain Ezra Noddy, that is. Guy I was talking to. Seems they called her father 'Squire.' Gives you the idea, doesn't it? This mansion—been there since the early eighteen twenties some time—is the 'new Towne place.' Go back to before the Revolution on Long Island, the Townes do. Royalists, probably, although Noddy didn't say."

"Bradley?"

"Married into it. About ten years ago. Married into the country club, too. Chairman of the membership committee. Drives a Rolls. Comes out weekends during the summer. Very fine gentleman. And I quote Captain Noddy."

"Does he know Mr. Bradley's dead, Tony?"

"Does now, anyway. Because I told him. Says it's very tragic. He was very active in community affairs, and it will be a great loss. Talks like an obituary in a small-town newspaper."

"Sound like very respectable people," Shapiro said.

"Pillars of the community, Lieutenant." Tony is appropriately formal within the confines of Homicide, Manhattan South.

"No—call it irregularities? In the—uh—mansion?"

"Nothing the captain's heard of. Or's talking about, anyway. Oh, there was an attempted burglary last winter. Amateur job, Noddy says. The Bradleys weren't there at the time. 'Not in residence,' way Noddy puts it. Either in New York or, possibly, somewhere in the West Indies. He doesn't rightly know. Nothing to do with us that I can see."

Shapiro said he couldn't see that it had either. He told Tony Cook where he would be at around ten and for as long thereafter as it took. Yes, about this TV show of Langhorn's. No, he didn't know that it would be getting them anywhere.

"I'll see if I can get anything out of these lawyers," Tony said.

"I don't suppose you will," Nathan said. "We never get much out of lawyers."

Or, visibly, out of anything else, Shapiro thought as the squad car moved slowly up Madison Avenue. Probably Frank Bradley had merely fallen out the window. That would make things simpler. Or, of course, he might have jumped. Possibly, he had invested all his money—or his wife's money?—in stocks which had taken a nose dive, and he had decided to dive after them.

That sort of thing did happen. A little before Nathan was born, the air had been full of unidentified falling objects.

The driver took the car off to find a parking place in a side street. Shapiro took the elevator up to the twelfth floor. There was a different receptionist behind the door marked "Folsom, Akins & Bradley." She would see whether Mr. Akins had arrived and whether he was free to see—?

Lieutenant Shapiro, New York police.

One moment, please. And if he would just have a seat?

"Mr. Akins has just come in. He has a little correspondence to look over. They'll call me back, Lieutenant. If you don't mind waiting a minute or two? There are magazines right beside you."

The magazines were *Reader's Digest* and the *Ladies' Home Journal*. Shapiro lighted a cigarette and finished it and was refusing himself another, when she said, "Mr. Akins can see you now, sir. Just straight along the corridor to the end. The name's on the door."

Shapiro walked through the typists' pool and along the wide corridor to the door marked "Mr. Akins." The door was closed and he opened it. The girl behind the desk said, "Lieutenant Shapiro?" and used the intercom. She said, "Lieutenant Shapiro, Mr. Akins," and got a grating sound back. "If you'll go right in, sir?"

The only trouble was that the girl was not Mrs. Sue Perkins. She was not in the least like Sue Perkins. She was several years younger. Also, she had long, deep-red hair. Shapiro looked at her for a moment. He said, "Mrs. Perkins isn't in today?"

"She was. Quite early, I understand. Then she—she had to step out. So I'm, well, sitting in for her."

"Is she expected back, do you know? I rather wanted to see her, as well as Mr. Akins."

"Oh, I'm sure she will be. She just stepped out, they said. Mr. Akins will see you now."

Nathan Shapiro went in to see Mr. Akins. Akins was wearing a darker gray suit today. It fitted him as well as had yesterday's lighter gray suit. He sat as erect and solid behind his desk as he had the day before. He said, "Good morning, Lieutenant," with a rising inflection in his voice.

"Just one or two minor points," Shapiro said. "I went downtown to see Mr. Langhorn yesterday afternoon."

Akins nodded his head gravely.

"The last person to see the poor old boy alive," he said.

"That we know of," Shapiro said. "Do you happen to know whether Mr. Bradley kept his office door locked, Mr. Akins? I mean the one to the corridor, not the one to his secretary's office."

"Sometimes, I suppose. When he especially didn't want to be disturbed. I really don't know, Lieutenant. I didn't—well, ride herd on him, you know."

Shapiro nodded his head sadly, to indicate that he did know. "So it might have been locked or unlocked yesterday afternoon, when you and he got back from lunch?"

"Yes. He went in that door. I've no idea whether he locked it after him. Miss Kline might know, I suppose. But she didn't come in today, they tell me. Called up to say she didn't feel up to it. Understandable, don't you think?"

"Very. Very upsetting experience she had. Quite— well, devoted to Mr. Bradley, I gather. Your own secretary, Mrs. Perkins, isn't in today either, apparently."

"Came in early and left almost at once, Lieutenant. Note on my desk saying she wasn't feeling well and had gone home and that she'd fix it with the pool. About this locked-door business. I get what you're after, of course. If it wasn't locked, anybody could have walked in and—well, pushed poor Frank. Anybody in the office. Or, damn near anybody, I suppose. We don't have any security here, of course. Nothing to secure, actually." He smiled. "Quite the reverse, our business is. We spread information, not lock it up."

"Anybody from outside would have to come by the receptionist, wouldn't they? Not just walk in?"

"They could have come in by the freight elevator, come to that. This end of the building. Across from my office, actually—other end of the short corridor."

"Somebody could come up in the freight elevator and not have to pass the receptionist's office. Do people ever do that, Mr. Akins?"

"I have a few times, when I came in off the side street. I suppose others may have. You say you saw this Langhorn yesterday? Because he was the last person to see Frank alive? Said he was alive when he left him, I suppose? Not be likely to say anything else, would he?"

Shapiro agreed that Timothy Langhorn could hardly be expected to say anything else. "He talked quite a lot about an option on some characters of his, Mr. Akins. Characters from a book of his. Feels—feels pretty violently—that Mr. Bradley didn't give him a fair shake. As far as money was concerned. Do you know anything about the rights of that, Mr. Akins?"

"That there was an option. Assigned to the firm when Frank joined it. Merged with it. That Langhorn was grumbling about it to Frank. It was Frank's baby, you see. A lot of fuss about nothing. Not worth the paper it's written on, actually. Been in our files for three years or so. Not a nibble. Writers—well, they dream a lot, Lieutenant. Get notions their characters are imperishable. That people are trying to steal them. Plagiarizing them. Hell, Lieutenant, they come a dime a dozen."

Shapiro said he saw. He said he supposed writers sometimes got exaggerated ideas as to the value of what they had written.

"And sue, sometimes," Akin said. "Even when they haven't got a prayer. Funny breed, writers. Even some of those who write copy for agencies like ours. Think writing copy is just—oh, a way of scratching out a living until they do something better. Bigger and better. Like a best-seller. Or a smash-hit play. Meanwhile, they scrape along on the thirty or forty a year we pay them. My heart bleeds for them, Lieutenant."

"Yes," Nathan said. "To get back to Langhorn. No sponsor for these books of his, as TV material, you say. Were you still trying to find one, Mr. Akins?"

"I wasn't. A couple of private detectives named Brook, weren't they? Something like that, I think old Frank told me. We just put this option agreement of his in the files and forgot it."

"Did Mr. Bradley forget it, do you know?"

"Apparently this Langhorn wouldn't let him. Oh, as a property—hell, he knew as well as I did that it was a washout."

"Didn't get somebody interested? Didn't plan to have a pilot film made?"

Akins leaned forward a little in his chair. He said, "What the hell, Lieutenant? Where the hell did you get that notion?"

"When I was down at Langhorn's apartment, a girl came in. Close friend of Langhorn's, I gathered. Said she had flown here from Hollywood because Mr. Bradley had offered her a part. Says she's an actress. Very pretty girl. Said the part was that of Enid Brook, and that Mr. Bradley had wired her to fly east because he was going to make a film about this Brook couple. Mr. Langhorn's characters, they'd be."

Akins said he'd be damned.

"You didn't know anything about this film, Mr. Akins?"

"I sure as hell didn't. Sounds like something this guy Langhorn dreamed up. Got this girl, whoever she is, to go into cohoots with him on."

"The girl's name is Peggy Claymore," Shapiro said. "That's what she said it was, anyway. Ever hear of an actress with that name, Mr. Akins?"

Akins said he never had. He said that, to him, it all sounded like some kind of funny business. He said, "If Frank had anything on the fire, he'd have told me about it. Hell, Lieutenant, we were *partners*."

"Sure," Shapiro said. "Probably this Miss Claymore, if she is a Miss Claymore, got things wrong, somehow. Mixed up. Anyway, it probably isn't important. Hasn't got anything to do with what we're interested in. Mr. Bradley's death. And probably I'm just taking up your time. You must have a lot of things to do, after what's happened. Still, I've got a job to do too, Mr. Akins."

"I suppose so. I mean, I realize you have. You want to ask some more questions? About what happened yesterday?"

"Yes. I'll try to keep it brief. You and Mr. Bradley got back from lunch about a quarter of three yesterday afternoon. Mind going over it again, Mr. Akins? Just so I'll get it straight in my mind."

"About that time. He went into his office and I went into mine. I've told you this, Lieutenant."

"Just to see if I remember it right. Langhorn went into Mr. Bradley's office around ten of three, Miss Kline says. Stayed maybe ten minutes. Spoke to Mr. Bradley as he was leaving, she says."

"I don't know anything about that, I'm afraid."

"The door between your office and Mr. Bradley's was closed, I take it."

"It's always closed. Unless one of us wants—wanted —to see the other about something."

"Locked ever?"

"Why'd it be locked?"

Nathan said he didn't know. He said he was just trying to get the picture. "About a quarter of three, you went into your office. Directly from the corridor? Or through Mrs. Perkins's office?"

"From the corridor. Always do."

"Yes. Then what, Mr. Akins?"

"Went over some correspondence I hadn't got to in the morning. Busy morning. Told you about that."

"Went over correspondence you hadn't got around to in the morning," Shapiro said. "For about how long, Mr. Akins?"

"Hell, I don't keep a stopwatch on myself, Lieutenant. Half an hour, maybe."

"During that time, you didn't hear anything from Mr. Bradley's office? Loud voices? Anything like that?"

"No. The door's pretty solid. And when I'm working I concentrate."

"All right. You went over your correspondence until, approximately, three-fifteen. Then?"

"Asked Mrs. Perkins to come in and bring her pad. She did, of course. I'd just started dictating when Miss Kline began hammering on the door. She was calling, too. 'Mr. Akins! Mr. Akins!' I said something like 'She sounds all worked up' to Sue. 'You'd better see what it's all about.' So, Sue went over and opened the door. And —well, you know why the kid was worked up. So Sue and I went into Frank's office and—I looked out the window, Lieutenant. Sue—I guess she tried to calm Miss Kline down. And I called the police. I didn't know what else to do."

He had done just the right thing, Shapiro told him. Shapiro stood up.

"By the way," Shapiro said. "When you were ready to start dictating yesterday afternoon. You used your intercom to tell Mrs. Perkins to come in?"

"Yes."

"When you called her on the intercom, did she answer right away? Come in right away?"

Akins did not answer immediately. He looked up at Nathan Shapiro, standing in front of him. He raised his eyebrows. He said, "Getting at something, Lieutenant?"

"Just the picture. To be sure I've got things straight in my mind."

"As a matter of fact, she didn't. I—well, I assumed she'd gone to the john or something. I had a cigarette and tried again. In about five minutes, probably. She answered and came in. She said something about she hoped she hadn't held me up. That she'd had to wash her hands. The way people do, you know."

Nathan said he did know. And he wondered if, offhand, Mr. Akins knew Mrs. Perkins's home address.

Akins said he didn't. He also said he hoped Shapiro wasn't going to bother Mrs. Perkins when she was apparently under the weather. Shapiro said he'd try not to, and who would know her address?

"Miss Drake. Dorothy Drake. She's office manager. Desk in the typists' pool area. As you go out. Desk has her name on it."

Nathan hoped he hadn't taken up too much of Mr. Akins's time.

"Tell Miss Drake I said it was all right to give you Sue's home address," Akins said. "We don't give them out usually. Rule against it, as a matter of fact."

Nathan promised to tell Miss Drake it was all right to give him Mrs. Perkins's address. He found Miss Drake where he had been told he would. She was a lean woman, probably in her late fifties. She had a thin face, dominated by a rather long thin nose. She said, "Yes?" in a thin voice when Nathan stopped in front of her desk.

Nathan told her what he wanted and about Leslie Akins's authorization. Although Nathan, a tall man, was standing in front of her, Dorothy Drake somehow managed to look down her nose at him. At least, it felt like that.

But she flicked through a card file on her desk. The address she gave him was in the Murray Hill district. He thanked her. She did not say he was welcome. She said, "Mmmm," thinly.

"By the way," Shapiro said, "was it you Mrs. Perkins told she wasn't feeling well and asked for somebody to take over for her? As Mr. Akins's secretary?"

"Certainly."

"About what time was that, Miss Drake?"

"A little after nine. Said she wasn't feeling well, so I sent Miss Kenny in."

"Mrs. Perkins had been to her office and then came back here?"

"I really don't know. I don't have to keep track of the private secretaries. Enough to do without that."

"I had the impresssion that Mrs. Perkins usually comes in just before Mr. Akins is expected," Shapiro said.

The telephone on Miss Drake's desk rang. She said, "Miss Drake speaking," and listened a moment and said, "Certainly, sir." She raised her voice a little and said, "Miss Romero. Art department." She put the receiver back in its cradle and looked down her nose at Shapiro and said, "Did you?"

Shapiro decided that that ended the conversation and took the elevator down to the lobby. His uniformed driver was waiting and said, "Just around the corner, Lieutenant. Won't take a minute."

Nathan went out and stood on the sidewalk in front of the building known as Twin Spires. It took almost five minutes. But it took only ten more minutes to reach the Murray Hill address in the East Thirties. It was an elderly house, rather like the one on Morton Street, only a little wider. But this one had the usual vestibule with the usual nameplates over the usual mailboxes and the usual bell buttons under them. Shapiro pressed the button under the box marked "Leon Perkins." From its location, Shapiro assumed the Perkinses occupied the first floor and, presumably, the semibasement under it. The "garden apartment," it would be called.

He was clicked in after only a minute-or-two delay. He went into a hallway with carpeted stairs rising out of it along the left wall. A man stood in a doorway at the inner end of the hallway. The man wore dirty white chino pants and a yellow polo shirt, and his belly strained both. He had a wide face and was almost completely bald. His forehead seemed to extend to the back of his neck. He was short, not over five feet three or four, and probably weighed well over two hundred pounds.

He said, "Yes?" as Nathan Shapiro, feeling needlessly tall and thin, walked toward him.

Shapiro said, "Mr. Perkins?" and stopped in front

of the man, who continued to block the doorway. He did say, "Yeah, I'm Perkins."

Shapiro said who he was and showed his shield to prove it. He said he'd like a word with Mrs. Perkins if she was up to it.

"Not here," Perkins said. "What do you mean 'up to it'? She's at her office. Folsom, Akins and Bradley. Only there isn't any Bradley anymore, she tells me."

"She isn't at the office," Shapiro said. "She left there"—he looked at his watch—"about two hours ago. Said she wasn't feeling well and was going home. She didn't, you say?"

"Probably she—oh, come on in. You can search the place if you don't believe me." He stepped back and to one side, and Shapiro went past him. Nathan felt that he sidled through, although that was not really necessary.

It was a big room they went into. The furniture was Swedish. It looked like a prosperous room. At the far end there was a Kovacs lamp lighting a desk and a typewriter. There was paper in the typewriter, and it appeared that Perkins had half finished typing on the sheet.

"Sit down somewhere," Perkins said. "Unless you really want to search the place, Lieutenant? Only you'll waste your time. Sue isn't here."

Shapiro sat down. The chair was much more comfortable than it had looked to be. Perkins sat in a larger chair, filling it—overfilling it.

"Have you any idea where your wife may be?" Shapiro asked him.

"Probably," Perkins said, "she's taking a long walk. Sue's a great one for long walks. Way she puts it, she walks things off. Walking off the—unpleasantness at the office yesterday, at a guess. Although Bradley's dying isn't going to break her heart, exactly. Mine either, come to that. Probably told you that yesterday. Open about things, my wife is. Too open, maybe. But that's the way she is. Hope she didn't give you any wrong ideas, Lieutenant. Like maybe I went around and pushed Bradley out of the window? Or even that she did herself?"

There was, Nathan thought, an almost bantering note in his voice.

"Only that she resented Mr. Bradley's firing you," Nathan said. "He did, I take it?"

"Revenge," Perkins said. "Smoldering hatred after —oh, two and a half years. Two years ago last February. You buy that, Shapiro?"

"At the moment," Nathan said, "I don't know what I buy, Mr. Perkins. You might, I suppose, say I'm pricing it."

Perkins chuckled; his whole bulging body chuckled. "Actually," he said, the chuckles still in his voice, "it was probably the best thing ever happened to me. Believe it or not. No more going to that damn office. No more pecking from above. From creative executive— that was Bradley—down to account executive and down to us, the guys who wrote the copy. Damn annoying. Not any of that now. Oh, a few 'wouldn't-it-be-better, Mr. Perkins, if—' But no real hard pecking. My line, they pretty much take it or leave it. Mostly they take it. And, I average out better than the agency paid me. So—no animus. No surging hatred leading to defenestration."

"Sounds very comfortable," Shapiro said. "What is your line now, Mr. Perkins?"

"Free lance. Free-lance copywriting. Means I work for myself. Not for some damn agency. Like—oh, in your field, I suppose like a private detective."

He paused. Nathan Shapiro made no comment.

"I'm supposed to have the light touch," Perkins said. "Sort of ironic, isn't it? Considering—oh, I saw the way you looked at me, Lieutenant. The way everybody does. Except Sue, I guess. Except Sue. 'Repulsive'—I suppose that's the word for it. The one that son of a bitch used, anyway. I wasn't supposed to hear it. Didn't, actually. But Sue did."

"What son of a bitch, Mr. Perkins?"

"Bradley. Who else? Three-four months after he—'came aboard' he always put it. Kind of cliché he was fond of. When he fired me because I look like a 'toad in pants.' "

"Fired you because you're—heavily built?"

"You put it nicely. When Sue and I were married I was—well, not as thin as you are, Shapiro. But, call it reasonably of a shape. It's glandular, my doctor says. So—"

"This work you do now, Mr. Perkins. Profitable, you say?"

"We're not starving. You're interested in that, Lieutenant?"

Shapiro said he liked to get the full picture.

"All right. No secret in the trade. You know Bryant and Washburn? Big store on Fifth. Specialty shops?"

Shapiro did. Everybody in New York knows Bryant and Washburn, even those who live in Brooklyn.

"I did a series for them a few months back. Just text. Ran in *Manhattan*. The magazine, you know. Around five hundred words or so. Written in the *Manhattan* style. Rather tricky, their style is. But—well, I'm up to tricks. Ten of the pieces. At a thousand a piece. Assignment directly from their advertising manager. Old girl named Ursula Fields. Great old girl. Mind you, I don't say the pickings are always that good. I do some work for agencies, too. Ones that want what they call the light touch and don't happen to have it in their stable."

"Folsom, Akins and Bradley?"

"No. Got offers once or twice. Not from Bradley, obviously. Told them no, with a few frills on it. You know what Bradley looked like, Shapiro? When he was alive."

Shapiro did not. He didn't know what Bradley had looked like dead, either. He was entirely satisfied not to.

"Richard Cory type," Perkins said.

Nathan shook his head.

"Man in a poem," Perkins said. "Poem by Robinson. 'Clean favored, and imperially slim,' Robinson said he was. Don't know how many emperors Robinson had run into. Always thought of them as rather rotund myself. Poetic license, I suppose. And a damned good line. Well, that's what Frank Bradley was. Wanted to be, anyway. Thought he was. And—wasn't tolerant of those who weren't. So—'repulsive.' It burned Sue up. More than it did me, as a matter of fact. She didn't go to the office for three days, and God knows how many miles it took her to walk it off. It was—well, demeaning to her too. That she would stay married to a freak—'a toad in pants.' There was that in it, of course. Don't think I don't know that. God knows I know that. The thing is —well, we love each other. Can you imagine that, Lieutenant? You met her yesterday. Can you imagine a woman like that loving—really loving—a man like me? Oh, the hell with it. None of your damn business anyway, is it? And God knows nothing for me to make a speech about."

People make speeches about what's biting them, Nathan thought. About what's gnawing at them. A thin, agile man lived in the blubber ball that was Leon

Perkins; a light and lively mind lived in that heavy head. And perhaps, for all he denied it, smoldering anger had lived there, too. Gone, now, with a man "clean favored, and imperially slim"—a squashed object on an autopsy table?

For all his weight, Perkins had moved easily, almost lightly, coming into the room. And he was heavy enough to be an almost irresistible force if he had occasion to push against something. Or somebody.

And Sue Perkins? Agile and quite strong enough, Shapiro thought. And absent from her office for at least five minutes. Perhaps, of course, for considerably longer than that. A decisive woman, she had seemed to be. One who would brood over a cruel remark, cruel to her—degrading to her—as to the man who said they loved each other; a man who made a point of it? You can't tell about people, Nathan thought. If he were cruelly hurt, would Rose feel pain as deep? Would what degraded him degrade her also? It was, he thought, a question he did not need to ask himself. Or Rose. When he got home, he would ask her if she knew a poem by someone named Robinson about a man named Richard Cory.

Sue Perkins had gone to wash her hands, she had told Leslie Akins. Perhaps she had. Perhaps she had felt a need to.

He became conscious that there had been a considerable silence while he pursued wandering thoughts. It was Perkins who broke it.

"I *was* working when you barged in," Perkins said. "And I've no idea when Sue will show up. You planning on waiting until she does, Lieutenant?"

"Sorry," Shapiro said. "I was just thinking things over. Trying to get them straight in my mind." He stood up. "No," he said, "I won't wait for Mrs. Perkins. When she comes in, ask her to give me a ring, will you?" He gave Perkins the telephone number of Homicide, Manhattan South. "If I'm not there, ask her to leave a message for me. Tell me where I can get in touch with her. O.K.?"

Perkins said, "Sure." Then he said, "Anyway, you didn't say 'contact.'" The bantering note was back in his voice.

Missing Persons? Shapiro wondered, back in the squad car. Or even an all points bulletin? Too early for either, of course. Too early for anything. Perhaps Tony had got something out of those lawyers. It seemed unlikely. Lawyers can be clams; usually are clams.

7

THE LAW FIRM of Kornfeld, Yarborough, Vincent & Goldstein had not been especially clammish, as law firms go. It was evidently a very large law firm, Tony Cook told Nathan. Very subdued and dignified. It, as represented by a somewhat starchy, gray-haired woman to whom Tony had been referred by the receptionist, admitted that it was legal consultant to the advertising agency of Folsom, Akins & Bradley. And counsel to Frank and Sylvia Bradley as individuals? Presumably, if they needed legal advice.

Had Mrs. Bradley, by any chance, had an appointment with one of the partners the day before?

"Began to shy away then," Tony said. "How did that information concern the police? Any information concerning a client was confidential. The old runaround. So I ran around." Finally—yes, Mrs. Bradley had had an appointment with Mr. Goldstein at noon the day before. Mr. Saul Goldstein. Yes, Mrs. Bradley had kept the appointment. At about one, Mr. Goldstein had gone out with Mrs. Bradley. Presumably to lunch. They had got back about two-thirty. Mrs. Bradley had stayed for about half an hour. No, Mr. Goldstein had not called his secretary in for dictation while Mrs. Bradley was in his office. Really, there was no way of knowing whether Mrs. Bradley had made a telephone call while in Mr. Goldstein's office. Yes, of course she might have.

"Goldstein?" Shapiro said.

"Not in, Nate." They were in Shapiro's small office, so "Nate" was all right. "Doesn't get in usually until eleven-thirty or thereabouts. Not expected until late afternoon today, if at all. In court. So there we are, I guess. Do we think it matters?"

"We are always curious," Nathan said. "Like it says in rules and regulations. No, Tony, it probably doesn't matter."

"I gave Miss Farmer a ring this morning," Tony said. "Made her overcook an egg she was poaching. About this part Bradley offered her."

Shapiro said, "Yes? And what did Rachel tell you?"

"A firm offer, she thought. As if things were all set, she thought."

"Other people around when he made this offer?"

"Look, if Rachel says he made an offer—"

"Yes, Tony. Don't be jumpy. Merely, was it all out in the open?"

"I asked her that," Tony said. He told Shapiro how it had been, including the drinks at the Carlyle. "She didn't get the impression that he was being *secretive* about it, Nate."

"He wasn't spreading it around," Shapiro said. "All the others—the ones connected with the agency, that is —were gone after Rachel had finished changing. Just

Bradley waiting for her. To take her for a drink at the Carlyle and offer her this part. Not much of a crowd in the Carlyle lounge at that hour, probably. Nice quiet place, I'd guess. They seem to know him there, did Rachel think?"

Tony hadn't asked.

"Sort of place for him, apparently," Nathan said. " 'Clean favored, and imperially thin.' What Leon Perkins says he was. Quotation from some poem."

"Richard Cory," Tony said. "Edwin Arlington Robinson."

Anyway, Nathan Shapiro thought, I'm pretty good with a gun. Damn good with a gun, actually. Which, just now, doesn't seem to apply.

"Perkins himself is a short fat man," Shapiro said. "Extremely fat. Very conscious of being. Says that's why Bradley had him fired from the agency. Because he is repulsively fat. The 'repulsively' was Bradley's word, apparently."

"He told Perkins that? To his face? Sounds like a thorough son of a bitch, Bradley does."

"That seems to have been a general impression, Tony. No, but in his wife's hearing. Sue Perkins's hearing, that is. And this morning, Mrs. Perkins left her office at a little after nine because she wasn't feeling well. Was going to go home, the office manager thought. Only she didn't. Hadn't got home a couple of hours after she left the office, anyway. Ten-fifteen minutes' walk from the office to their apartment. Great one for walking, her husband says she is. Likes to 'walk things off,' when there are things to walk off. Walked a lot after Bradley fired her husband for being repulsive, according to said husband."

Tony Cook said, "Mmmm."

"He's averaging out better than what the agency

paid him. He said. Seems to me Mrs. Perkins told us he isn't getting half as much—something like that."

Tony said, "Mmmm," again.

"Yes," Shapiro said. "She probably left the office this morning shortly after I called in and arranged to see her boss. And, Tony, she wasn't in her office yesterday at a little after three. Akins called her on the intercom and she didn't answer. Came in a little later, he says, and told him she'd gone to the ladies' room to wash her hands. Let's go have some lunch, Tony. Then, I guess, we'll see if we have better luck finding Miss Kline."

They had sandwiches at a nearby delicatessen. Tony had a beer to wash his down; Nathan drank milk. They got a taxi to take them to the address in the East Thirties. The building was, again, a town house converted into flats. Nate found "Kline—Brown" in one of the vestibule slots. He pressed the button under it. Nothing happened. After half a minute, he pressed it again. The proper grating squawked at him. It sounded slightly like "Yes?"

"Miss Kline? Lieutenant Shapiro. And Detective Cook. We'd like to see you for a few minutes. About what happened yesterday."

The grating did not squawk. But there was a rather loud clicking in the lock of the inner vestibule door. Tony pushed the door open, and they went up one flight. It was Amelia Kline who opened a door for them. She looked, Shapiro thought, as if she had missed last night's sleep. He said, "You're feeling all right today, Miss Kline?"

"I'm all right," she said. "Better, anyway, I guess. Come on in and—ask your questions." They went on in. The room was not large; it was rather scantily and routinely furnished. That morning's *New York Times* was on the floor by one of the chairs. There was an ashtray on a small table on the other side of the chair. It was filled with cigarette butts. "It looks dreadful," Amelia Kline said. "We rent it furnished, Mary and I do. Mary Brown. We share it. I look awful too, I guess." She ran slender fingers through short black hair. She nibbled at almost colorless lips with small white teeth. She said, "Can I get you something? Coffee or something? Or a drink. There's sherry, I think. But I'm afraid it's cooking sherry."

They didn't want anything.

"Well," she said, "I do. If you'll excuse me a minute?"

She went while Nathan was saying, "Of course, Miss Kline." She went through a door at the end of the room and closed it behind her.

"Taking it hard, isn't she?" Tony Cook said.

Shapiro said she did seem to be taking it hard. "Nasty experience for a kid her age," he added. "Unpleasant at any age, of course. And, I'd think, she didn't regard Bradley as a son of a—"

He stopped, because the slim dark girl came back into the room. She carried an earthenware mug, holding it in both hands. She had smoothed her hair, so that now it was a black cap on her small head. She had put on lipstick—put it on, Nathan thought, with care. She put the mug down on a table beside a chair and sat on the chair. She drank deeply from the mug which, Shapiro could see, held very black coffee. She took a tissue from the pocket of her skirt and touched her lips with it. Then, again, she drank from the mug.

"I'm sorry," she said. "I forgot to have any breakfast. Anyway, I think I did. I'm all right now, Lieutenant. And Mr. Cook. Or should I say, 'Detective Cook'?"

"It doesn't matter," Tony said, and thought that

Amelia Kline was still a shaken young woman and that she seemed even younger than she had the day before. And now, with her hair smoothed, and lipstick on, even prettier.

"You can go ahead now," she said. "I'm all right now. I just needed coffee, I guess."

"Yesterday," Nathan said, "when Mr. Akins and Mr. Bradley came back from lunch, Mr. Bradley went directly into his office? Not through yours? Is that right?"

"Yes. He almost always did."

"Was your office door—I mean the door to the main hallway—open when they came back? I mean, you could see them when they walked past it?"

"Oh, yes. I got up and closed it after I could hear that Frank was in his office." She did not this time, Shapiro noticed, correct the "Frank" to "Mr. Bradley."

"Mrs. Perkins's office is right next to yours," Shapiro said. "When you went to close your door, was her door open, do you remember?"

"Yes, I think so."

"And was she in her office?"

"I don't—yes, she was. I heard her typing and looked in, and she—oh, sort of waved. And looked at her watch and shook her head. And then I closed my door and went back to work. On what Mr.—on what Frank—had dictated in the morning. The memo I told you about. The one to Mr. Parker about the Lusterglow text."

Shapiro nodded his head. "An advertisement that a Miss Farmer—Miss Rachel Farmer—had posed for, Miss Kline?" Tony asked her. "Posed for photographs, that is?"

Amelia Kline was sure she didn't know. She said, "That would be art department, you see."

Tony said he saw.

"About then," Shapiro said, "when you got back to typing this memo, you got the call that Mr. Langhorn was outside, was early for his appointment. And said he could come on in if he wanted to."

"Yes." She drank more coffee.

"And he did come in and after a few minutes went into Mr. Bradley's office. And stayed there only a few minutes. And spoke to Mr. Bradley as he was going out?"

"I told you all that yesterday."

"I know you did. We have to go over things a lot, I'm afraid. To be sure we get them straight."

She nodded her head. Then, again, she drank deeply from her coffee mug. And, again, she dabbed at her neatly colored lips.

"Just to make sure I have got things straight," Shapiro said. "After Mr. Langhorn left, a few minutes after, Mrs. Bradley called and wanted to speak to her husband. That's right, isn't it? That would have been about a quarter after three, since Mr. Langhorn was in Mr. Bradley's office such a short time. I am getting it straight?"

"Yes. Oh, I wasn't looking at my watch, you know. But that sounds about right. Then I tried to reach him and—" She stopped. She was holding the coffee mug. She put it down on the table. It shook in her hand and clattered a little when it touched the table top.

"We don't need to go over that again," Shapiro told her. "After Mr. Langhorn left, before Mrs. Bradley called, did you hear any sounds from Mr. Bradley's office? Movement? Voices? Anything?"

"No. The door's heavy. Solid. I never hear anything from in there when it's closed. I can hear people walking in the hall sometimes, through my other door. Just—

oh, the sounds of their feet. And sometimes, if they're talking, their voices. Not what they're saying, usually. Just voice sounds."

"Yes," Shapiro said. "Yesterday. Before Mrs. Bradley called. Did you hear any sounds from the hall? People talking? Or walking?"

"I don't think—no, wait a minute. I think I heard Sue close her door and then—walk along the hall. I guess I know the way her heels sound on the floor. It's— well, it's a noisy floor. Tile or something, I think."

"Could you tell which way she was walking, Miss Kline?"

"No, of course not. Only, we're at the end of the hall, you know. There's really only one way to walk."

"Except, of course, into Mr. Akins's office. Or Mr. Bradley's."

"She'd go through her own door to Mr. Akins's office. She wouldn't go out into the hall and in his other door."

"To Mr. Bradley's?"

"Why would she go into Frank's office? Anyway, she wouldn't without coming through my office to have me find out whether he was free. I—I just heard her walking. I didn't pay any real attention. Why should I? I suppose I thought, if I thought about it at all, that she was going to what Frank always called the 'head.' He used to be in the Navy, you know. In the Navy they call it the head. What we call the—the washroom. Frank went to Annapolis. The Academy, he always called it. He was something called a 'j.g.' when he resigned his commission. Wait. A lieutenant, junior grade, was what he was. He showed me a picture of himself in—in uniform once. He looked—"

She buried her face in her hands and for a moment her body shook with sobs. But they were soundless sobs, and almost at once she took her hands down from her face. She reached down and took the coffee mug in both her hands. Then she stood up.

"I'm sorry," she said. "I'm terribly sorry. I think I'll get—I think I need some more coffee."

Her voice was husky. As she turned from her chair, her first step seemed uncertain. It was almost as if she stumbled. But then she walked, steadily and rather quickly, down the room and out through the door at the end of it. She did not quite close the door behind her. For a moment, they could hear her muffled sobbing. Then another door closed.

"In love with her boss?" Tony Cook said.

"It happens," Nathan said. He lighted a cigarette. He got up and found an ashtray. It, too, had butts in it. The butts were long. Cigarettes had been stubbed out almost as soon as they were lighted.

"Yes, Tony," Shapiro said, "I suppose we'll have to find out."

They had to wait longer this time. It was more than five minutes before Amelia Kline came back into the room. Again, she carried the coffee mug carefully in both hands. She had, Nathan thought, redone her face. She had, in a sense, redone herself. She was composed, now. She even managed something like a smile as she put the mug down and sat in the chair beside the mug's small table. She took an almost empty pack of cigarettes out of her skirt pocket and shook a cigarette out of it. Tony flicked his lighter and reached it across to her. She said, "Thank you, Mr. Cook."

Then she looked away from Tony Cook and at Shapiro. She spoke slowly, in a carefully steady voice. She said, "I don't know what you must think of me, Lieutenant—think of my acting this way."

"I think you were fond of Mr. Bradley," Shapiro said. "Perhaps very fond."

"I thought you would," the girl said. "I'm not very good at hiding things, am I?"

Neither of them answered what was not a question.

"We were going to get married," she said. Her voice was very tight; stretched tight.

"Frank and his wife had agreed to get a divorce," she said. "She—she was going somewhere—Reno, I suppose—and file. Then Frank"—her too tightly held voice broke for an instant—"then Frank and I were going to get married."

"This divorce," Nathan said. "They'd decided on it because Mr. Bradley wanted to marry you?"

She shook her head.

"It wasn't just that," she said. "We, Frank and I, weren't breaking up—well, a happy marriage. It hadn't been that for years. Actually, it had been a mistake from the start."

"Mr. Bradley told you that, Miss Kline?"

"Yes, of course. But I knew it was true. She stayed almost all the year at that place of theirs out on Long Island. Her place, really. 'Her kind of life,' he told me once. 'Not my kind.' "

"She came into town in the winters," Tony said. "That's what we're told, anyway. Went on winter vacations together."

"Almost never together," she said. "Not while I've been working for him, anyway. He has—had—a house in Key West. He'd go there, usually in late January, and stay until around the first of March. He kept in touch with the office, of course. I'd send down whatever was important. You see, Mr. Akins usually takes his vacations in the spring. Goes up to Canada, I think, and fishes for salmon. The way they'd worked it out, Frank told me."

"And Mrs. Bradley?"

"I don't know. Stayed in town and went to the theater, maybe. With somebody, Frank thought. He didn't care. Last winter, I think she went on a cruise or something. I told you I've never met Mrs. Bradley. Didn't I tell you that?"

"Yes, Miss Kline, I think you did."

"Anyway, last winter I knew she wasn't at that big apartment of Frank's. And he said something about her being on a cruise ship. With a—with a friend. In January and part of February, that was." She paused. Then she said, "Oh." Then she drew deeply on her cigarette.

Neither of them asked her how she knew that Sylvia Towne Bradley had not stayed in the New York apartment the winter before. Or whether Frank Bradley had made his usual trip to his house in Key West, Florida. It didn't seem relevant. Or necessary.

"We have to pry into a lot of things which aren't really pertinent, Miss Kline," Shapiro said. "I'm sorry. Just a few more questions. Do you happen to know whether Mr. Bradley had any contacts with a Mr. Birnham?"

"Oh, yes—Mini-Motors," she said. "Mr. Akins was the one who showed the clients the renderings, almost always. After Frank and the account executive and the copywriters and the art department got them up. But Frank had a good many contacts with clients during the creative stages—conferences, phone conversations, memos, and so on."

Her voice was a little less tight, now. She ground out her cigarette and drank from her coffee mug. She took the cigarette pack out of her pocket and looked into it and shook her head and put it back. Like most of us nowadays, Tony thought. With the pants scared off of us. And the Administration saying, "Let's go easy on this clean-air business for a while, huh? Not really good for the free-enterprise system." Tony lighted a cigarette. He felt, vaguely, that he was violating national security.

"Do you know, Miss Kline, whether Mr. Bradley has been in touch with a scriptwriter recently? I mean, somebody from outside the office. About—oh, writing little scenes for TV commercials? Dialogue, I mean. That sort of thing?" He groped in his mind briefly. "Mother and daughter having a little conversation about how hard it is to get to sleep sometimes. And that something or other relaxes you and isn't habit-forming and that you can buy at any drug counter without a prescription? You know the sort of thing I mean."

"Our copywriters do that sort of thing, Lieutenant. Not people from outside. Oh, if we—if Frank and Mr. Akins—produce a TV movie for some sponsor—yes, then a scriptwriter comes into it, of course. We don't, very much. Independent producers do that sort of thing mostly. And try to sell pilots to the networks. And we sell them to sponsors. I think that's the way it is. Of course, sometimes it gets complicated. Everybody in on the act, you know."

Shapiro didn't. He nodded his head anyway.

"But a few weeks ago," she said, "Frank did have an appointment with a man named Anderson. Roy Anderson. He was in Frank's office quite a long time, and Frank said something about their going over a script. To explain why I had to tell so many people he was busy for so long."

"Going over a script," Shapiro repeated. "For a TV film, would you think? A pilot, that is."

She didn't know. Neither did she know where they could get in touch with Roy Anderson, who might be a scriptwriter. She did have his address and telephone number in her card file at the office.

They had come up with some information suggesting the agency was planning to make a pilot film using characters created—Shapiro was getting rather tired of that word, but one had, apparently, to learn this strange language—by Timothy Langhorn. Did Miss Kline know anything about that?

She took the cigarette pack out of her pocket again and looked into it again. This time she shrugged slightly and put the cigarette between her lips. Tony again reached a light to her. She drew deeply and blew smoke toward the ceiling. Then she said, "No, Lieutenant. Not that I know of."

"If such a project was in the works, you'd probably know about it, wouldn't you, Miss Kline? As Mr. Bradley's private secretary? His confidential secretary?"

For the first time, there was a trace of a smile on Miss Kline's wan face. "I guess I should take that back," she said. "Though I wasn't really in on it. Frank would get pretty—oh, hush-hush about a project—a deal—that wasn't concluded. What he called finalized. Was superstitious about it. He might drop a hint—without meaning to, you know—and then he'd say it was too soon to discuss it. Would write his own memos—that sort of thing. Even after we decided to get married." The smile vanished, but she went on. "About Mr. Langhorn's characters, all Frank would tell me was that he was 'negotiating.' But I couldn't help getting—inklings. Like the business about a script with Mr. Anderson."

"A few days ago, Miss Kline, did you send a telegram for Mr. Bradley to a Miss Claymore—Peggy Claymore? In California, somewhere. Hollywood, probably."

"The actress?" she said. "No, Lieutenant."

"Apparently she got one," Shapiro said. "Asking her to fly back. Saying he had a part for her."

"No, Lieutenant. I never sent that kind of wire to Miss Claymore. Since you say she got one, Frank must have sent it himself."

"But you do know she's an actress, apparently."

"She was in a play last winter. Frank took me to it. It didn't get good notices and didn't run very long. But we both thought she was very good. Much better than the play. That's all I know about her."

It wasn't much; none of this looked to Nathan Shapiro like being very much. Things to wonder about, of course; things to speculate about. He stood up. Tony Cook hesitated a moment before he, too, stood. Shapiro said, "Yes, Tony? Something you'd like to ask Miss Kline before we go along? And let her get some rest?"

Tony hadn't been sure there was anything he wanted to ask Amelia Kline. But, yes, Nate did have second sight sometimes.

"I just wondered," he said, "whether Mr. Bradley had a separate telephone on his desk? A direct line, I mean. With its own number. So that he could call out, and people could call him? Without going through the office switchboard? And through your office, of course?"

"Oh, yes," she said. "A direct line. With an unlisted number. Mr. Akins has one too. And the head of the art department, I think."

Tony said he'd just been wondering. Shapiro said, "Thank you, Miss Kline. I'm sorry we have to put you through this sort of thing. I realize it is harrowing for you."

"I want to help," she said. "Any way I can, I want to help." She hesitated. She said, "You're quite sure—

116

the police are quite sure—that Frank didn't merely—fall? Lose his balance or something?"

"We're not really sure of anything about it," Shapiro told her. "Just trying to make sure, Miss Kline." He took one step toward the door and stopped and turned back. "By the way," he said. "One other thing. I take it that Mrs. Bradley didn't know this unlisted number of her husband's direct phone. Since when she called yesterday she went through the switchboard and your office."

"That's what she did yesterday," the girl said. "I don't know whether she knows the other number. Or perhaps, I suppose, she does know it and yesterday just forgot it. And couldn't look it up, of course, because it's not in the book."

Shapiro agreed that that was possible.

On the street again, they found a telephone booth which wasn't marked Out of Order. Leon Perkins's number was not unlisted. When Shapiro dialed it, there was no answer for a good many rings. Finally, Perkins answered it. He said, "Yes?" in the voice of a man unfairly disturbed. He said, "No, she hasn't. I said I'd tell her you wanted her to call you when she does show up." With that, he hung up.

8

THEY TOOK A CAB back to 230 East Twenty-first Street, where Homicide, Manhattan South, is lodged with the Thirteenth precinct in the Police Academy building. The building is relatively new and relatively air-conditioned. They went to Shapiro's small office off the squad room.

"Could be she didn't decide to walk things off," Nathan said. "Could be she took a taxi somewhere."

Tony agreed it could be. It also could be Mrs. Sue Perkins had walked to Forty-second Street and taken the subway to somewhere. Or a cross-town bus. Or, for that matter, a train to Albany. It could also be that she had merely gone to a movie and was now having lunch somewhere. Or she might merely have gone shopping. Was it important?

"We don't like people merely taking off," Nathan told him. "Sure, she may have done anything. Vanished into thin air, for all we know. However, let's start where we have one chance in a thousand."

"M.P.B.?" Tony said.

"Too soon," Shapiro said. He reached for his telephone and got an outside line. He dialed the number of Folsom, Akins & Bradley and asked for Miss Dorothy Drake. Her voice was just as thin and hard on the telephone as it had been across her desk. "Yes, Lieutenant? I'm quite busy just now."

Shapiro was sure she was, and he wouldn't take a minute. When Mrs. Perkins saw her that morning, said she wasn't feeling well, and asked for a temporary substitute as Mr. Akins's secretary, did Miss Drake happen to notice what she was wearing?

A gray dress. One she often wore. Well, she'd call it light gray, if that meant anything. Yes, long sleeves, of course. A coat of any kind? In this weather? No, no hat. "She's not the kind who wears hats, Lieutenant," with the inflection of one who did. Oh, certainly below her knees. Did he think Sue Perkins was the kind to wear a miniskirt? No, she didn't know about the shoes. Did he think that she had nothing better to do than to stand up behind her desk and look at people's shoes? Black handbag, she thought. She couldn't be sure. And what on earth was this all about?

"Just routine," Nathan Shapiro told her. It is an answer as noncommittal, and as unrevealing, as "No comment." He thanked Miss Drake and hung up.

Taxicab drivers in New York City are required by law to keep trip records. Those who drive for fleets turn them in at the end of a day's tour. Morning drivers usually knock off between four and five in the afternoon, depending on how close to the home garage they happen to be. Independent drivers are supposed to keep their trip records available. There are non-medallion drivers, who are not supposed to cruise for fares. And who often do. There are some thousands of taxis cruising New York streets except, of course, when you want one. A thousand to one against was optimistic. However—

Shapiro put it in the works, which would mean tedium for a lot of New York City policemen. Pickup from in front of, or near, a Madison Avenue office building known as Twin Spires. Subject: Female, middle-thirties, height five feet four or five; wearing a long-sleeved gray dress; probably carrying a black handbag; brown, short hair; no hat. Where dropped?

"There are a couple of hundred Andersons in Manhattan alone," Tony said, emerging from the Manhattan telephone directory. "Five Roys. Three just 'R.' One of the Roys is in Harlem. One's in Christopher Street, which sounds more likely somehow. Could be Bradley reneged on her, couldn't it? Said, Sorry, I've changed my mind. Think I'll stay with my wife, instead. And go on being chairman of the membership committee at the club. Might have upset Miss Kline if he said something like that."

"I think it would have upset her a good deal, Tony. But, that much? And maybe, Mrs. Bradley wasn't all that amiable about a divorce. We only know what Miss Kline tells us Bradley told her. Could be Mrs. Bradley was really sore as hell."

"Could be Bradley just fell out the window," Tony Cook said. "Could also be he jumped."

"Yes," Shapiro said.

He looked at his watch. It was nearly four. They were running out of day—not of their day, which was uncomfortably subject to extension. The day they were running out of was the conventional nine-to-five day; the office day. And they didn't seem to be getting anywhere. They had not even established that there was anywhere to get. Frank Bradley could, indeed, merely have fallen out his open window. What they had so far accomplished was to lose a witness. And possibly a witness to nothing.

They could, of course, drop the whole thing; report accidental death. I could also resign, Nathan thought. He clawed his way out of the slough with which he was too familiar.

"Picture of Mrs. Perkins," he told Tony Cook. "Her husband will have one. Get it spread around, huh? Then try the Christopher Street Anderson. Then, God knows what."

Tony said, "Right." He could see his seven o'clock date fading in the mist. He said, "You'll be here, Lieutenant?" and stood up. Nate was down again, from the sound of his voice. But sometimes Nate sounded most doleful when he was beginning to get a hunch—to get a feeling about a setup. Tony Cook wasn't getting any feeling at all, except that they seemed to be just splashing around, not even stirring up the waters.

"No," Shapiro said. "With any luck, I'll be talking to a man named Birnham. At something called the Mini-Motors Corporation. And don't ask me why."

Tony was tempted to advise Shapiro to snap out of it. He did not. He said, "Sir," which would give Nate the idea, and went back to his desk in the squad room. He looked up the number of Perkins, Leon, and dialed it. After six rings, he got "Yeah?" in a very grumpy voice. When he identified himself, he got "What now, for God's sake? Damn it, man, I'm trying to get some work done."

"So am I," Tony told him. "Has your wife got home yet? Or have you heard from her?"

"No. For all I know, she's still walking. Or's gone to a movie. I don't keep a string on her. She'll show up when she wants to."

"You're not worried, Mr. Perkins?"

"Hell, no. She can take care of herself. Has been doing it for years. What's all your hurry?"

"We want to talk to her. We're investigating a murder case."

I guess we are, Tony thought.

"Also," Perkins said, "you're driving me nuts. You and this Shapiro. I told him I'd have her call. What more do you want, Cook?"

"At the moment, a picture of her, Mr. Perkins. We're trying to find her, and a picture might help."

Perkins said, "Je*sus* Christ." He said, "You're making a hell of a fuss about a woman's going for a walk. To walk something out of her system. She does it all the—"

"A picture, Mr. Perkins?"

Perkins guessed so. He'd look around, and if he found one he'd put it in the mail, if Cook would tell him where—

Tony said he'd be around to pick it up. He checked a squad car out and went around.

Leon Perkins was just as much a blubber ball as Nate had said he was. His face was too broad and soft to show much expression. But his eyes, Tony thought, were worried eyes. He had not one but four pictures of Sue Perkins ready on a table. He said, "There you are. You're sure as hell making a lot of fuss about this. Sue's all right, I tell you."

And telling yourself, Tony thought. And trying to make yourself believe.

One of the photographs was of head and shoulders, professional and, at a guess, fairly recent. There was no animosity in the pictured face, as there had been in the face Shapiro and Tony had seen the day before. "One of the art department boys took that one," Perkins said. "Pretty good of her. Way she is now."

The other pictures were snapshots. One showed her on a beach in a bathing suit. Her figure was better than Tony had realized it was the day before. Another was of Sue Perkins with a man not as tall as she—a plump, smiling man, recognizable only after a moment's scrutiny. Both were smiling.

"A while back," Perkins said. "When we were younger and I didn't look the way I do now. Better crop me out, if you want that one."

Tony didn't want that one. He took the head-and-shoulders photograph and promised Perkins would get it back after they had some copies made.

"The thing is," Perkins said, "she'll be along any minute—probably."

There was not, Tony thought, any real confidence in his voice. It hung a little on the "probably."

"Sure she will, Mr. Perkins," Tony said. "Sorry we had to bother you."

Unexpectedly to himself, he held his hand out. Perkins took his hand. Perkins's hand was firmer than Tony had expected it to be. It was also damp. Nervous tension makes hands sweat. Perkins wasn't, Tony thought, really managing to convince himself that his wife would be along any minute.

Tony took the photograph to the nearest precinct to be put in the works—to be copied many times and

123

to be distributed to many precincts. And to be shown, they could hope, finally, to some taxi driver—or change-booth man in a subway station or somebody at a ticket window at Grand Central—who would say, "Yeah, seems like maybe I remember a dame looks something like that. Seems like maybe she—" (Was the one I picked up sometime after nine this morning. The one I sold tokens to, although who looks at them? The one who bought a coach ticket to Buffalo this morning.)

Tony looked up and dialed the number of Anderson, Roy, who had an address on Christopher Street, in the Village.

* * * * *

Mr. Birnham would see Lieutenant Shapiro now. If Lieutenant Shapiro would come this way?

"Now" was fifteen—no, twelve—minutes before five o'clock in the afternoon. "This way" took him out of a large room on the twentieth floor of a new, mostly glass office building on Park Avenue, where mansions had stood once. Well, but before Nathan's time, mansions had stood on Fifth Avenue, too. Nathan followed a very trim young woman, whose rear wobbled hardly at all, between glass doors which had opened voluntarily at their approach, and along a wide corridor to a wooden door, which did not open of itself. The trim young woman rapped briefly on the door and opened it and said, "Lieutenant Shapiro, sir," and stepped aside.

Shapiro went past her into a large, light room, with deep orange carpet on the floor. At the far end of the room, at least thirty feet from the door, there was an outsized desk—about the size of a billiard table, Nathan thought, with a dark man in a dark suit sitting behind it. He was sitting in a high-backed chair the color of the carpet. The man, whose black hair was long and carefully styled, did not say anything. He merely watched as Shapiro walked—plodded was more like it —through long-haired carpet up the room. He was only a few feet from the desk when the man spoke. He said, "You're a police lieutenant, I understand. Name of Shapiro, they tell me."

The elegance cracked slightly as he spoke. There was a subtle trace of accent in the words. Faintly, it reminded Shapiro of his father. Rabbi Shapiro had never quite eliminated accent from his English, although he was a learned man. Rabbi Shapiro's German had been excellent. So, Nathan had been told, had been his father's Hebrew. Nathan had had to take that evaluation on faith.

"Yes, Mr. Birnham," Nathan said. "Shapiro. Attached to Homicide. About Mr. Bradley. I understand you knew him?"

"Businesswise, yes," Nathaniel Birnham said. Elegance collapsed entirely. "He and Mr. Akins handle part of our advertising. Have for some years. Is somebody supposed to have killed Bradley? I gathered he had just fallen out of his office window. The one he kept open."

"That's what killed him," Nathan said. "We're trying to find out how he came to fall. I gather you've been in his office, Mr. Birnham? Since you know about the window."

"I wasn't in it yesterday," Birnham said. "Sit down, if you want to. Although I can't give you much time."

There were two straight chairs on Shapiro's side of the desk. Neither of them had a high back. Shapiro sat on one of them.

"I'll try not to take long," Shapiro said. "And I didn't suggest you saw him yesterday, Mr. Birnham. But—sometime recently? Last week or so, perhaps?"

"Not at his office. Here at mine, of course. Three or four days ago. So?"

"To discuss an advertising campaign?"

Birnham for several seconds regarded the smooth, uncluttered top of his desk. He moved, slightly, a slender vase which held four orange marigolds. The orange of the flowers did not quite match the color of the carpet and the chair. Even an executive vice-president and advertising manager can't have everything, Shapiro thought. Flowers go their own way, show their own colors.

Birnham nodded at the flowers, approving them. Then he said, "Yes, Lieutenant. We're—well, let's call it expanding our advertising program. We specialize in small cars, you know. We feel that this is the time of small cars. Compacts. Luxury with economy, you understand. Comfort combined with—intimacy, if you know what I mean. Hence, Mini-Motors. Ten years ago it was the Majestic Motors Corporation. Now it's the Mini-Motors Division of. Have to keep abreast of the times, eh, Shapiro?"

Shapiro curbed the inclination to say he wasn't in the market for a car. He said, "This expanded campaign, Mr. Birnham. Does it involve the use of television?"

"Certainly. Best way to reach the market. Damn near the only way, nowadays. Oh, a few magazines still. *Manhattan,* for example. The rendering for *Manhattan* was what Akins showed me yesterday morning. But for us, sure, it's television more and more. We don't need an agency to tell us that."

"What kind of television advertising were you and Mr. Bradley planning on?" Shapiro asked.

"Folsom, Akins and Bradley," Birnham told him. "Why do you ask that, Lieutenant? I mean, trade secrets, you know. Does Macy's tell Gimbels?"

Nathan hadn't heard that one in years. He doubted that anyone had. His long sad face lengthened.

"I'm not a competitor," he said. "I'm a policeman. Trying to find out whether somebody pushed Mr. Bradley out a window. You're a law-abiding citizen, willing to help the police. Anxious to help the police."

"Sure," Birnham said. "And how will details of our advertising campaign help you? Nothing settled yet, anyway. Negotiations going on. Not—well, not at the tops of our voices. Not being shouted from housetops."

Apparently Birnham could always find time for a cliché. Nathan said he could understand Mr. Birnham's position. He said he had no intention of shouting from housetops.

"Did this campaign you and Mr. Bradley were working on involve a series of short movies for television, Mr. Birnham? Involving some characters named Brook? Based on characters in a mystery novel? By a man named Langhorn? Timothy Langhorn?"

"Where did you get that idea, Shaprio?"

"Let's say I found it floating around," Nathan told him. "Something like that was involved, I take it?"

Birnham's marigolds needed looking at. They needed very careful looking at for several minutes. Then Birnham looked, instead, at Nathan Shapiro. Finally, Birnham seemed to make up his mind. He said, "Suppose it was?"

"You and Mr. Bradley had discussed it? Talked about terms, things like that? Perhaps Mr. Bradley had shown you a script for this—I believe you call it a pilot film, don't you? As a basis for a possible series?"

My God, Nathan thought, I'm beginning to learn the language. I probably speak it with an accent.

"We hadn't got that far," Birnham said. "Nothing signed, you understand. Nothing definite. Hell, they haven't got even a time segment lined up with a network. You don't just call up a network and say you want eight-thirty to nine-thirty on Tuesdays for thirteen weeks. They're fussy as hell about ratings. Don't you know that, Lieutenant?"

"I don't know very much about the advertising—business," Shapiro said. He had almost said "racket." It was probably just as well he hadn't. Probably Nathaniel Birnham thought of it as the advertising "profession."

"It was altogether preliminary, I take it," Nathan said. "Just something you and Mr. Bradley were talking over?"

"He did have a synopsis some scriptwriter had come up with," Birnham said. "All right, showed it to me. Folsom, Akins and Bradley showed it to the Mini-Motors Division of the Majestic Motors Corporation. More accurate way of putting it. Not just Bradley and I. And—well, things like this can take months to finalize, you know."

Shapiro nodded his head. He said he realized that, of course, it was a matter of negotiations between firm and firm, not between man and man. That Frank Bradley was only representing the agency of which he was a partner. And, by the way, had Mr. Akins taken part in any of these preliminary discussions?

"No. Bradley was the creative director. Worked out the overall ideas. Akins will come in when we get

128

things set. Would have, I mean. Take over from poor Bradley now, of course. Unless he gets a new partner in. Probably will. It's not a one-man operation, his isn't. Fifteen percent of—well, of a lot of millions, Lieutenant."

Nathan nodded his head, hoping the movement showed proper awe.

"Just an idea," he said, and stood up. "An idea and a synopsis. That's right?"

Birnham said that that was right. He did not stand up.

"There's just one other thing," Shapiro said. "I somehow got the idea that this option—the option Bradley had on Langhorn's book, the characters in the book, anyway—is about to run out. That you and the agency haven't got months to work things out. Only until the first of September was the idea I got somewhere."

Birnham told his marigolds that he had no idea where Lieutenant Shapiro had got that idea.

Neither the flowers nor Shapiro told him. Shapiro did say that he appreciated Mr. Birnham's cooperation and that he hoped he wouldn't have to bother him again.

It was twenty minutes after five by then. It was five-thirty by the time Nathan found a telephone and called in. No taxi driver had been found who had picked up a five-foot four—or five—woman wearing a long-sleeved gray dress and no hat in front of Twin Spires on Madison Avenue and dropped her somewhere. The day-shift hackers were still checking in at their garages. No man, or woman, at a subway token counter, had recognized the photograph of Mrs. Sue Perkins. Nobody behind a ticket counter at Grand Central remembered selling her a ticket, to anywhere.

Not yet did anybody remember any of these things. And, no, Detective Anthony Cook had not yet called in.

Lieutenant Nathan Shapiro left word that he would be home if needed. He wedged himself into a subway bound for Brooklyn. It was the middle of the rush hour. He hoped that he could reach his station before he reached suffocation. It would be a close thing. It always was.

9

Tony Cook let the telephone listed for Roy Anderson, of Christopher Street, ring seven times. It was not answered. Tony hung up and got his dime back. It was, he thought, his first lucky break of the day. Sometimes the New York Telephone Company merely swallows dimes without even saying thank you. Tony looked at his watch. Five-thirty. If he took a taxi—with no chance of putting the fare on an expense account—he could get home and shower and change and ring the doorbell in Gay Street by seven. Or, he could walk to the nearest IND subway station and get off at Fourteenth Street. Probably be faster that way.

And probably the Roy Anderson in Christopher Street wasn't the Roy Anderson he wanted. Probably he was a Roy Anderson who worked nine to five in an office somewhere, not a Roy Anderson who wrote movie scripts. Probably he merely hadn't got home yet.

Tony started walking. With any luck, he wouldn't find a telephone booth in working order before he got to a subway station. After all, his shift had been finished for an hour and a half—an hour and thirty-eight minutes, actually. He was supposed to be off duty. But, damn it all, so was Nate. And Nate wouldn't have knocked it off. Goddamn it to hell.

He had walked three blocks when he came to a telephone booth. It would have an Out of Order sign on it, probably. It didn't have. His luck was running out, Tony thought. Not that it had, on that Tuesday in July, especially run in. He put his dime in the slot and got the tone and dialed.

Roy Anderson's telephone rang five times. Not home yet. So, with the consciousness of duty attempted if not done, Tony could—

In Anderson's apartment, the telephone was lifted out of its cradle and the ringing signal stopped. Nothing else happened. Nobody said anything. When Tony said "Hello" several times, with increasing loudness, he was not answered. He listened and, faintly, could hear voices. Several voices, it sounded like. But none of them projected into the telephone.

Somebody had got tired of the telephone bell and picked the telephone up and laid it down, probably on a table. Well, that was one way of stopping the annoying jangle of a bell. A damned incurious way; not a nine-to-five office worker's way.

So, Tony thought, and stepped out of the booth. A taxi with its top light on was less than a hundred feet away. All right, Tony thought, I'm a detective and the regulations say I'm supposed to be curious. "Always curious." He flagged down the cab. He explained to the hacker, who obviously worked the Bronx—or possibly

Queens—where Christopher Street could be found. He said, "Your light was on, pal," in answer to the driver's annoyed insistence that he had been just about to go off duty. "Go down Fifth to Ninth and I'll guide you." He shut the door, ignoring the sign on it which said, "Please do not slam door."

When the hacker said, "Listen, Mac," Tony showed him the shield. The driver said, "O.K., if that's the way you want it, Mac."

They went down Fifth Avenue to Ninth Street. The traffic was heavy. The hacker was expert—New York taxi drivers have to be to stay alive—but it still would have been faster to take an IND train to Fourth Street. But what the hell? Seven o'clock was shot, anyway.

Ninth Street from Fifth to Sixth Avenues was jammed with cars, standing still and with their horn rims leaned on, in a pointless effort to incite the car stopped at Sixth to jump the red light. Or simply fade away. When they had inched halfway down the long block, Tony said, "O.K., you can let me out here." The hacker said, "Look, officer. You said Christopher Street. This ain't Christopher Street." Tony told him that this would do, anyway, and paid him off. The driver said, "O.K. Mac, but it ain't Christopher Street." He put his Off Duty sign on just in time to thwart a broad woman who had thought, momentarily, that the age of miracles had not passed.

By the time Tony reached Sixth, the now off-duty cab was only seven cars away from the red light. The light changed for Tony, and after he had waited for five cars to turn up Sixth, he made a run for it. The cab didn't make it on that light. Probably by now the hacker thought he was never going to make it back to the Bronx. Or Queens.

Tony walked along Christopher looking for the number, which would be on the uptown side of the street. He walked by the sign which said "Gay Street" but not without looking, a little wistfully, down Gay.

The number was that of what had, presumably, once been a loft building. Anderson's residence in it—on the third floor—was probably only marginally legal. Not one of the laws Detective Anthony Cook was required to enforce. If there was a law. Tony climbed two flights of stairs.

A door which would have to be Anderson's was open. It was open on a large room which seemed to be full of people and cigarette smoke. Tony went into the room. There is little point in knocking on an open door. Nobody paid any attention to him.

The big room, almost the building wide and all of the building deep, was not really full of people. Ten people—no, eleven—sat on straight chairs, roughly in a circle. They were of assorted sexes. Each of them held a sheet of paper, in some cases several sheets. A lean man, who looked young but had a bush of white hair, was in the center of the circle. At first, it seemed to Tony that the man was jumping up and down. Then Tony realized that the man actually was standing almost still; he merely seemed to emanate motion.

He had his back to Tony. He was facing a young woman on the far side of the circle. She faced Tony. The young woman was Rachel Farmer, and she had her mouth a little open, as if she were about to speak. Her eyes were very wide open, in astonishment. Tony supposed his own were too.

"From the *top*, I said," the lean, white-haired

man said—shouted. "Snap out of it, Gloria. Snap *out* of it! You're not dead yet."

"You're wrong," Rachel said. "Terribly wrong. Somebody's been lying about me. Lying, I tell you."

She spoke in a flat voice, without any emphasis at all. She did not look at the sheet of paper she held. She looked down the room at Tony, her eyes still wide.

"For God's sake," the lean man said, despair in his voice. "Maybe you *are* dead, girl. Listen, will you? Just *listen!*"

He said again what Rachel had just said. There was, in his reading, no lack of emphasis. "Lying, I tell you" came out almost as a scream. He said, "Listen, girl. This guy's going to kill you. Strangle you with his bare hands. You're scared stiff. Those are the last words you'll ever speak and you know it. You're not, for God's sake, reading back to the boss from shorthand notes." He stopped, and stared at Rachel. Then, in a much quieter voice, he said, "I know this is just a read-through, Miss Fulmer. But you're not reading statistics. Or something out of a cookbook. And—"

"My name is Farmer, Mr. Anderson," Rachel said. "And I don't know shorthand. Also, the police have arrived."

"The hell they have," Anderson said. "Sirens. Murderer climbing out the window onto the fire escape. Blah, blah, blah from the sponsor. *Then,* the police arrive. You've had a copy of the script all afternoon, Miss Whatever-your-name is. Didn't you ever find time to glance at it?" He paused, obviously for timing, Tony realized. Then, in a tone of loathing, Roy Anderson said, "*Amateurs!*"

"No," Rachel said. "Not your policeman, mister. A real policeman. Right behind you. Hi, Tony."

Tony said, "Hi, dear," and Anderson whirled to face him. Anderson also said, "What the hell?"

"Sorry to interrupt your rehearsal, Mr. Anderson. Miss Farmer is right. I am a policeman. Anthony Cook, Homicide Squad, Manhattan South. But go ahead with your rehearsal. I'm in no hurry."

He wasn't, now.

"Not a rehearsal," Anderson said. "A read-through. So I can tell how it sounds. Not how it reads on paper. There can be a hell of a lot of difference sometimes. The way I work, Mr.—sorry, I didn't get it."

"Cook, Mr. Anderson. Detective Cook. Homicide Squad. Working on a script for a film based on Timothy Langhorn's characters, I take it? A pilot for a possible series? For the advertising agency of—"

"Yeah. This guy Akins gave me a ring late this morning. Said to get on with it. That it was all set, in spite of what happened to—all right, guys, take a break. Get yourselves coffee or something, if you want it. Back there." He gestured toward the rear of the long room. "And don't drink up all my booze."

The admonition was a friendly one.

The circle broke up. There was some milling about. Several of Anderson's cast drifted toward the end of the room where the coffee was, and where booze was to be treated with discretion. One who went was a slender, noticeably graceful young woman with a suggestion of red in her blond hair. Familiar? Yes. A girl in a play he and Rachel had seen a while back. A girl Rachel had thought he looked at too intently. Couldn't think of her name at the moment.

"What happened to Bradley, you were going to say, weren't you?" Tony said to Roy Anderson.

"Yes. What brings you here, I gather. Why here, Cook?"

"We get around, Mr. Anderson. Here to see if you were working on a script for this pilot film we've been hearing about. The one you've been working on with Mr. Bradley."

"Not *with* anybody," Anderson said. "Bradley told me they wanted a pilot script—made-for-television sort of thing—based on these characters of somebody named Langhorn. I said I'd do it. Talked it over with him, sure. But it's my script."

"He suggest the casting?"

"Yes. Oh, he was going to produce it. Said he'd probably direct it, too. No idea whether he can direct, but that's not my problem, is it? Oh, sure, I'd like to see it get the ratings. Be turned into a series. Get a chance at some of the scripts, of course. Way I make a living, you know."

"You've been working on this script for some time, probably?" Tony said.

"Not so damn long. Couple of weeks, actually. All at once a great rush about it. Wanted it like yesterday. Way these advertising jerks are sometimes. Think they'd know better, wouldn't you? Hell, I'd never read this Langhorn's books. Never heard of Langhorn, come to that. This dame Enid Brook of his is kooky. Talks like it. Picked up some of her dialogue from the books. Cleaned it up a little, so it'll read."

"You can do that? I mean, legally? It isn't plagiarism, or something?"

"You nuts? The agency owns the rights. Probably paid Langhorn a whack for them."

"From what we hear," Tony said, "they've owned their rights for some time. Several years, we understand. Bradley had them before he joined up with Akins, way we get it. Why all the sudden rush, do you know?"

"No. Not my problem. At a guess, they all at once hooked a sponsor. But Bradley didn't tell me what the big hurry was. Just that they wanted a working script like yesterday. So, they've got the script, or damn near. Soon as I hear how it sounds."

"You used the story, the plot, from Langhorn's book, I suppose?"

"From one of them. Called it *Brook No Evil*, Langhorn did. Not much of a title, for my money. So these detectives are named Brook. So what?"

Tony said he didn't know.

"Had to pep it up some," Anderson said. "The story line, I mean. Maybe all right to read, Langhorn's job is. But it wouldn't play. Had to put some bang into it."

"And it's ready now? With the bangs in it?"

"Automobiles," Rachel said. She had not joined the others for coffee. Or Mr. Anderson's booze. "Chasing each other. Knocking each other off roads. Catching fire. You see, I have read the script, Mr. Anderson. Even if you did give me only a couple of hours."

"As much time as anybody had, Miss Fulmore."

"Farmer, mister."

"Fulmore. Farmer. Whatever it says on the list, sister."

Rachel didn't say anything.

"Anyway, Gloria's only got a couple of sides. In the teaser she gets killed. Flashback, she has these cocktails with this Ned-boy. Says she'll never leave him. That this time it's for keeps. Blah, blah, blah."

"Only two blahs," Rachel said. "Just blah, blah. I think she ought to say more."

"So you want to rewrite it, do you? *Actors.*"

His inflection on "Actors" was what it had been on "Amateurs." It had been similar when he spoke of "advertising jerks."

Tony said he wanted to get one or two things straight. Leslie Akins had called Anderson up that morning and told him they were all set. That Frank Bradley's death wasn't going to hold things up. Was that right?

"Told me to get cracking. That he wanted to see the script tomorrow. Show the final draft to a client. I told him I wanted a read-through first. Way I always work. But I couldn't start it before four."

"You had the cast lined up?"

"Week ago, we knew who we wanted, Bradley and I did. Had to get this Claymore chick back from the Coast. Got in yesterday, she did, Akins told me. And gave me her phone number. So, I got on the telephone. Claymore yelped a bit. Something about having a dinner date. I said, 'Look, baby. You've flown back from L.A. to get a job. You want the job?' She quit yelping, I'll say that for her."

"He called me around one-thirty, Tony," Rachel said. "Said to get here by four. I'd been posing all morning and was bushed. But I got here by four."

"Almost," Anderson said.

"Well, almost. And since then, we've all been sitting around reading lines at each other." She paused for a second. "And I'm still bushed," Rachel Farmer said. "And it must be getting on for seven, Tony."

Tony looked at his watch. Actually, it was getting on for six-thirty. But he took her point.

"I take it you two know each other?" Anderson said.

"As they say, it's a small world," Tony said. "Yes, Miss Farmer and I know each other."

"Who the hell says it's a small world?" Anderson asked him.

Tony couldn't, offhand, recall that anybody recently had. He said that it had been good of Mr. Anderson to have let him interrupt things and that Mr. Anderson had been helpful. He looked at Rachel.

"O.K.," Anderson said. "I'll stand in for her. Read her lines, since she's so bushed. But tomorrow morning at nine. O.K., Miss Fulmore? Complete read-through, so I can mark it up and get it up to this Akins guy by noon, way he wants it."

"All right, Mr. Henderson," she said, and stood up. Anderson grinned at her.

"All right, Miss Farmer," he said. "You'll do, by the way. Maybe another time, if it runs to a series, we can manage something fatter. Maybe with four blahs in it, even."

Rachel said, "Thank you, Mr. Anderson," and she and Tony walked down to the street together. It still wasn't seven. On the other hand, he hadn't had time to get his shower and the day's second shave.

* * * * *

It was cool in the Shapiros' apartment in Brooklyn —well, reasonably cool. Nathan had his gun off and his jacket off before the telephone rang. Rose was bringing in two tall glasses on a tray. One held her evening, hot-weather, gin and tonic. The other was Nathan's sherry on ice with a splash of soda. In summer, Nathan yields to his wife's insistence on something long and cold. She has tried to convert her long, sad husband to something less sweet, but has only got him as far as sweet sherry on ice. She regards this as a small advance over sweet red wine without ice. She put the tray down and answered the telephone. She said, "Yes, Tony, he is. Just got in."

So, Anderson had been the right Anderson; Akins was in a hurry for a script based on Langhorn's characters, and Anderson had it almost done. All but a final read-through to find out if it sounded all right. O.K., probably typescript didn't always translate smoothly into the spoken word. Which wasn't something Nathan Shapiro would know anything about. So Rachel had been one of those reading lines for Roy Anderson.

"Convenient," Nathan said. Tony Cook agreed that it was convenient. Tony did not know whether Timothy Langhorn had been told Akins was picking up the option. No, Tony needn't bother. No doubt Miss Claymore had already passed the word to Langhorn, who'd have to take the bird in hand, apparently. He might be wistful about the one his agent discerned in the bush. On the other hand, he might think that five thousand would be an adequate bird.

"It would to me," Tony said. Nathan agreed that five thousand would also be a largish bird to him. Yes, if Tony wasn't at home or at Miss Farmer's, he'd try Hugo's French Restaurant. He hoped he wouldn't have to try.

Oh, and the sponsor who'd been acquired by Folsom, Akins & Bradley, now diminished to Akins Associates or something, probably was the Mini-Motors Division of the Majestic Motors Corporation. It was nothing that need bother the New York Police Department.

No, nothing had come through on Mrs. Sue Perkins.

New York City is a large haystack. Hay was being diligently turned over. O.K., they'd start again in the morning.

Nate went back to his drink and to Rose.

"I was afraid you were going to have to go out again," Rose said. "I wish we could just take the receiver off. I had it off for a couple of hours this afternoon."

"You're a civilian," Nathan told her. "Still on Trollope?"

"I switched over to Jane Austen," Rose said. "Pampering myself, I suppose. Now I suppose I'd better get out to the kitchen."

Nathan shook his head slowly.

"All right," Rose said. "I'll consider my arm twisted, dear. For the rest of our drinks, anyway. It's going to be broiled fish. I'll have to sit up with it."

They drank, slowly, relaxed. It had been years since they had needed speech to ensure tranquillity. Rose lighted a cigarette. Prompted, Nathan lighted one too.

"Did you ever hear of a man named Cory?" Nathan asked her, a little to his own surprise. "Richard Cory, I think it is."

"If you mean the poem, yes, dear. 'Clean favored, and imperially slim'? The one you mean? And whatever—?"

"Somebody mentioned him today," Nathan told her. "Indicated somebody was like him."

"Very elegant, if so," Rose told him. " 'A gentleman from sole to crown,' and widely envied. And 'went home and put a bullet through his head.' On a 'calm summer night,' too."

"He killed himself? Why, does it say?"

"No, Nathan. The poem doesn't say. To—oh, to suggest that desperation may lie under a polished exterior, maybe. Poems don't have to spell things out, dear. They don't even have to say anything at all. Feeling things is enough for poems. And—oh, singing in your mind. Who was like Richard Cory, Nathan?"

"A man who's dead," he told her. "As dead as Richard Cory."

"Did he die in the same way, Nathan? Oh, if you're talking about this Bradley man, I know he fell out a window, wasn't shot. But, another way of doing it, Nathan?"

"We don't think so. It's hard to be sure one way or the other, but we don't think so."

"If he was like Richard Cory," Rose said, "I'd think he'd have taken a neater way."

"There isn't any really neat way," Nathan said, his voice very sad. "Shooting yourself can be very messy, too."

Rose said that they were getting moody, and that she thought they needed another drink. She went out to get them. This time she mixed Nathan a very light gin and tonic. She believes that sweet wine is a depressant. Nathan Shapiro noticed, but he did not protest. He went back to sorting things out in his mind. Things didn't sort.

They were just finishing their drinks when the telephone rang.

* * * * *

Rachel said she thought being an actress was going to be fun and that the others in the cast seemed like nice people.

"Not condescending," she said. "Because they're

143

professionals and I'm not. Only, I'll have to join the Screen Actors Guild, Tony. It's a closed shop, Mr. Anderson says, so I have to be in it. Your Miss Claymore is a very nice person, I think. Not snooty at all."

"*My* Miss Claymore?" Tony said, and held a Tio Pepe bottle poised over the chilled glass. It was the second chilled glass. It was cool in her apartment, and she insisted she didn't feel bushed anymore. "No, not mine, child. Wrong size. Wrong color."

"All the same, you looked at her. I saw that, mister. However, I think you'd be out of luck, anyway. I think she has other ideas. This writer. Not Mr. Anderson. The other one. The first one. She calls him Tim."

Timothy Langhorn, Tony told her. The man who had invented the characters Anderson was using in his script.

"Not invented, Tony. Created. That's what they call it."

"All right. Created. What makes you think he's Miss Claymore's other idea? She say so? Like, 'Timothy Langhorn is my own true love?' "

He poured into the chilled glass. He dropped ice cubes into a squat glass and poured a little bourbon on them. He carried the filled glasses to a table and sat beside her on the sofa while she was saying, "Of course not, Tony. 'True love,' indeed. You make her sound like an Irish tenor. The way she talked about her lines. As Enid Brook. That's the part she's playing. I was a little late getting there, actually. She was talking to Mr. Anderson. When I went in, she was saying, 'But she doesn't *sound* like Enid, Mr. Anderson. It's not the way Enid talks.' As if this Enid were a real person. Then she said, 'You've lost what Tim put in her. Now she sounds

—well, like just anybody.' And Mr. Anderson said he'd just cleaned the lines up a little. 'To make her vaguely coherent, Peggy,' was what he said."

She sipped from her glass. Tony looked at her and waited.

"That's all, really," Rachel said. "It was as much the way she said 'Tim' as anything."

Tony said he knew what she meant. He added, "Rachel."

"We haven't had dinner yet," Rachel Farmer told him. "Yes, that's what I mean, Tony. Then she waved these sheets of paper at him and said to come on and she'd show him. Try to give him the idea, she said. So they went off to a little table and put the papers on it and began, I guess, to go over them. It was her part, of course. Carbons, actually. And pretty smudgy. At least mine was."

"She was showing him changes she thought he ought to make?"

"The way it looked to me. They were too far away for me to hear. Anyway, I was reading my own part. In the cocktail lounge before I get strangled. It's a flashback. Somebody saw us, me and the man who kills me, having drinks, and starts to tell Mr. and Mrs. Brook, and then it fades to a flashback. There's something in the scene that gives them a clue, you see. The man who kills me is named Raymond. I never call him Ray. That's what makes the Brooks wonder. Gets them on the case, actually."

Tony said he saw, in a tone which made her laugh. He said, "I take it the 'you' is Gloria?"

"I live my parts," Rachel said, with the inflection of one who quotes. "Are we going to dinner? Because maybe I'm a little bushed."

Tony finished his drink and stood up. He held his hands down to her, not really because she needed to be helped out of the sofa. She took them, not because she really needed help.

Then the telephone rang.

10

Tony got to East Twenty-first Street before Nathan Shapiro. Gay Street is closer to the Police Academy building than Brooklyn. Tony was lucky in finding a cab on Sixth Avenue, and traffic, at a few minutes after seven, wasn't too heavy. Nevertheless, he had time to wonder, as he occasionally did, whether he had been wise in his choice of occupations. The nine-to-fivers had some solidity in their lives. When they were through for the day, they were through for the day. Telephone calls didn't jangle in on them. They had, among other things, time to eat dinner.

Rachel had said that it was perfectly all right and that she was a little bushed anyway and that she would scramble herself some eggs and study her part. "All four lines of it," she had added. And, all right, it was a damn nuisance. She was getting used to it, but that didn't mean she had to like it.

On the other hand, Tony thought as he paid off

the driver, I tried a nine-to-five job when I was a kid, before I decided to go on the cops, and it bored me stiff. I'm not cut out to be a company man. All the same, damn it to hell. Now and then, when he's on the eight-to-four, a man ought to have a chance to plan his evenings.

He resisted the inclination to walk a block and grab a sandwich. Nate had said as soon as he could make it. He went up to the second floor.

The man waiting beside his desk in the squad room was small. He wore a black mustache which was obviously too large for his face. He was smoking a cigar. He had also been eating it. It didn't, to Tony, smell like a good cigar.

Tony said, "Mr. Arnez?" and sat down at his desk. Manuel Arnez, fleet taxicab driver, according to what Nate had said, blew smoke at him. It was really a noxious cigar. Arnez said, "Yeah," and managed to say it with a heavy accent. "I been off duty for two hours and I ain't had no dinner."

"Neither have I," Tony said. "But this shouldn't take long. You recognized this woman from a picture you were shown, way I get it. A woman you picked up at—"

"Listen, Captain," Arnez said. "I ain't swearing to nothing. All I told this guy she sorta looked like. Far's I'm gonna go."

"O.K.," Tony said. "We aren't asking you to swear to anything. You were cruising up Madison Avenue this morning and this woman flagged you down. All right, maybe this woman. Somebody who looked like the picture." He took the picture he had got from Leon Perkins—the picture which had been so many times copied and so widely circulated—out of the drawer of his desk. "This picture."

Manuel Arnez looked at the picture. He ate some more cigar. He said, "Yeah. That's the picture. But I ain't swearing to nothing. Got a match, Captain?"

Tony gave him a folder of matches and watched him light the stub of the cigar. (A cigar toward which Tony was beginning to feel a rather intense animosity.) Arnez blew smoke at Tony.

"You think this picture may be one of the woman you picked up this morning, Mr. Arnez? On Madison a couple of blocks below Forty-second?"

"Could be. Maybe. Like I said—"

"I know what you said. You're not swearing to anything. About what time was this?"

Arnez took a folded sheet of paper out of his pocket and unfolded it—a trip-record sheet from a cabdriver's clipboard, Tony realized.

"Twenty after nine, says here," Arnez said, refolded the sheet, and put it back in his pocket.

"Picked her up at nine-twenty," Tony said. "A woman in a long-sleeved gray dress. No hat. Carrying a black handbag. That right?"

Arnez took the cigar stub out of his mouth and looked at it.

"Look," Arnez said, "I know you guys. Pushing people around. People who ain't done nothing."

"All right," Tony said. "We're pigs. But I'm not pushing you around. Make this easy, Mr. Arnez, and we'll both have some dinner. You picked up a woman who maybe was the woman we're asking about on Madison Avenue about nine-twenty this morning. Where did you let her out?"

"Fifty-seventh and Park. Far side of Park, she wanted. Had to wait for the light. And then she came up with a ten-spot. Hell, I'd just gone on duty. What did she expect, huh?"

"You couldn't change it?"

"Took all the singles I had. So suppose the next one comes up with another ten-spot?"

"Things are tough all over," Tony said. "Did your next fare come up with a ten-spot, Mr. Arnez?"

"No, he didn't. And you know what he tipped? A lousy two bits. This lady was more like it. Half a dollar. Usually, it's the other way around, if you know what I mean."

Tony did. It is a confirmed belief of taxi drivers that women are worse tippers than men.

"The way I get it," Tony said and stopped because Nathan Shapiro came into the squad room. He looked at Tony Cook and Manuel Arnez and nodded his head and went on toward his office. Tony told Arnez to wait a minute and followed Shapiro. In his office, Nathan looked like a man who had been deprived of his dinner. But, of course, he usually looks as if he had been deprived of something.

Yes, the taxi driver had said Fifty-seventh Street. Didn't Akins live on Fifty-seventh Street? And yes, Mrs. Perkins had probably been his passenger. Tony went back to the squad room and told Arnez that that would be all, and that they would get in touch with him if they needed to and that they appreciated his cooperation. Arnez said, "Yeah?" with an inflection of complete disbelief, and put the soggy remnants of his cigar in the tray on Tony's desk and went away.

The cigar was loathsome. It had, however, gone out. Tony picked up the ashtray, holding it at arm's length, and dumped it in the trash container most distant from his desk. He went into Shapiro's office.

They agreed that Fifty-seventh Street might well be a coincidence. From the far side of Park, Mrs. Sue—probably for Susan, but they didn't know—Perkins might have walked anywhere on Fifty-seventh. Or, for that matter, to any place up or down Park. Or, conceivably, on to the East River and jumped in. But sleeping coincidences are not like sleeping dogs. They got a squad car and drove uptown.

The address Captain Fremont and Detective Latham had got from Leslie Akins, as a matter of routine, was that of a tall and evidently new apartment house on the south side of Fifty-seventh. It had a uniformed doorman. A doctor had his plaque by the entrance. Inside, in the cool lobby, there was a counter with a uniformed man behind it and a switchboard behind him. He had been sitting on a stool. He stood up and looked at them and said, "Can I help you, gentlemen?"

Shapiro said, "Mr. Leslie Akins?"

"I'll see," the man said. At least, Nathan thought, he didn't say he would ascertain. "Whom shall I say is calling?"

Nathan told him who he should say would like to see Mr. Leslie Akins. The man looked at them and raised his eyebrows. Neither Shapiro nor Cook said anything, and the man plugged into the switchboard. He waited less than a minute and said, "Mr. Akins, sir?" and that a Lieutenant Shapiro and a Detective Cook would like to see him. He listened for a moment and turned back.

"Mr. Akins is just going out," he said. "He asked whether tomorrow won't do. At the office, he says."

"Tell him we'd like to see him this evening," Nathan said. "And that we won't keep him long."

The man told Akins. All right, they were to go right up. To Penthouse A. That elevator.

"Lot of security," Tony said in the elevator. "And we seem to be getting penthouse clientele this time around."

Nathan said that, the way things were nowadays, security made sense. He added that they also had basement clients this time around.

Although Tony had pressed the button marked "Penthouse," the elevator stopped at the twenty-first floor. They walked up a flight of stairs and found two polished wooden doors. Tony pressed the bell in the jamb of the door with "A" on it. The door opened almost at once, and it was Leslie Akins who opened it. He was as erect and substantial at home as he had been in his office. He said, "Just caught me, gentlemen. Mrs. Bradley and I were about to go out to dinner. But come in, gentlemen."

They went into a large room, the far wall of which was largely glass. Tony thought that he was, this time around, running into a good many people who lived in glass houses.

Sylvia Towne Bradley was sitting by a coffee table. There was a sherry glass in front of her. She looked younger than she had when Tony had last seen her in her, or her husband's, glass penthouse. She had, he thought, gone to more trouble with her makeup. She wore a dark blue summer suit and high-heeled shoes of the same color. She was elegant this evening, Tony thought. She still looked as if she belonged in the country.

"A couple of detectives, Syl," Akins said.

She looked at them. She nodded her head slightly. She said, "I've met Detective Cook." Her intonation did not indicate that it had been a pleasure.

"Shapiro," Nathan told her. Her expression did not really alter. Perhaps it set a little.

Akins suggested that they sit down. They did. He went to a chair near the coffee table and picked up his glass. The liquid in his was darker than the liquid in

Sylvia Bradley's. Akins was still drinking dry manhattans, Tony thought.

Akins did not offer drinks. He said, "Yes, gentlemen?"

"We're still trying to get in touch with your secretary, Mr. Akins," Nathan said. "Not having any luck, I'm afraid. Can't find anybody who's seen her since she left the office this morning because she wasn't feeling well."

"She was going home," Akins said. "You're sure she didn't? You try that husband of hers?"

"Late this afternoon," Tony said. "An hour and a half ago, about, she hadn't got home. Her husband's getting worried about her. Says he isn't, but I think he is."

Akins shook his head slowly. Sylvia Bradley got up, unhurriedly, and picked up her glass, which was almost empty, and carried it to the glass side of the room. There was a terrace beyond. She was, Tony thought, signaling both her complete lack of interest in the whereabouts of Akins's secretary and her readiness to go out to dinner.

"You seem particularly anxious to get in touch with Sue, Lieutenant," Akins said. "Mind telling me why? Surely you don't think she—" He did not finish.

Shapiro gave him several seconds to continue. When he did not take advantage of them, Shapiro said, "She's conceivably a witness, Mr. Akins. In connection with our investigation of Mr. Bradley's death. We don't like witnesses to simply disappear."

He looked at Mrs. Bradley when he mentioned her husband's name. There was nothing to indicate she had heard the name. Or the word "death." She had withdrawn. It was almost as if she had left the room.

"You still haven't explained why you've come

here," Akins said. "I gathered from what you told the man downstairs that it was a matter of some urgency. Mrs. Bradley and I have been discussing the future of the agency. Now that she's a part of it. As I said, we were about to go out to dinner."

Nathan said, "Part of it?" He looked across the room at Sylvia Towne Bradley. She was still taking no part in anything; was not concerned with any of it. She continued to look out at Manhattan. She did finish what remained in her glass.

"Of course," Akins said. "Syl inherits Frank's share, naturally. His partnership. We've been—well, planning the immediate future of the firm."

"It will go on as before, Mr. Akins? With Mrs. Bradley as your partner instead of her husband?"

"Not quite like that," Akins said. "Mrs. Bradley hasn't had any experience in advertising, have you, Syl?" She did not answer. Again it was as if she had not heard. "We'll have to find somebody to take old Frank's place, and that won't be easy. Somebody who's heading up his own agency now, maybe. But he'd probably want to merge. Somebody who's working for another agency— hell, a man as good as we need would want the earth. Of course, he might bring an account with him. Unless his contract ties him up. Frankly, it's a bit of a problem, Lieutenant. But, not yours, is it? Probably boring you with this inside-the-office stuff."

"No," Shapiro said. "I'm not bored, Mr. Akins."

"Nothing to do with poor Frank's death," Akins said. "Not that I can see, anyway."

"Probably not," Shapiro agreed. "Of course, it isn't always easy to tell what may be involved with what. But you're probably right."

"You still haven't answered my question, Lieu-

154

tenant. Why did you come here this evening? In, I take it, the course of your search for Mrs. Perkins?"

"Because we have reason to believe Mrs. Perkins took a cab uptown this morning," Shapiro told him. "From in front of your office building to Fifty-seventh and Park. About half a block from here."

"And you wondered whether she had come here. To my apartment. Whether I'm—what, Lieutenant? Hiding her?"

"Earlier today," Shapiro said, "we gathered you didn't know until you got to your office that Mrs. Perkins was—taking the day off. Because she wasn't feeling well. Her husband assumed—says he assumed, anyway—that she had gone, as he says, 'to walk things off.' Was that what you assumed, Mr. Akins?"

For the first time, Sylvia Bradley seemed to be interested in what was being said. She turned toward them. There was still no expression in her deeply tanned, faintly sun-marred, face. Akins lifted his glass. He emptied it in one long swallow. He put the glass down.

"I did know Sue sometimes took long walks when things worried her," Akins said. "This morning I didn't think about it one way or the other, that I rem—" He stopped in the middle of the word. He lifted his glass again, but found it empty. He got a pack of Kents out of his jacket pocket and shook a cigarette out of it and lighted the cigarette. He lighted the filter end, and it flared. He crushed the fire out in a tray. He did not light a new cigarette.

Nathan Shapiro merely waited.

"All right," Akins said. "Maybe I wasn't entirely sincere with you this morning, Shapiro."

Nathan assumed he meant "truthful"; that he was

talking in a still unfamiliar language. Nathan waited. When Akins seemed to have difficulty in choosing further words, Nathan said, "Go on, Mr. Akins. Mrs. Perkins did come here?"

Slowly, Leslie Akins nodded his head.

"She was very upset," Akins said. "I've never seen her so upset before. About—about nothing, really. I—well, I just wanted to help her, you see. Give her a chance to pull herself together. Before—well, before you started badgering her with more questions. I could tell from the way she sounded on the phone that she needed a chance to—call it get organized. So I told her to come on up."

"You telephoned her this morning? At the office? Before you went down there yourself? Was that the way it was?"

"No. Why would I have called her? She called me. I was just having coffee. About—oh, a quarter after nine, at a guess. I usually get to the office about ten, you see. And stay until God knows when. Left earlier than usual this afternoon. Syl—Mrs. Bradley, that is—and I had arranged to meet here at six. To talk things over."

People wander. Sometimes, but by no means always, to avoid coming to a point. A point which might prick.

"Mrs. Perkins telephoned you about a quarter after nine," Shapiro said. "You were having coffee. Were you alone, Mr. Akins?"

"Kumi was in the kitchen. Unless he'd already gone. He was off today—"

"Kumi?"

"Man who takes care of the place. Takes care of me, I suppose you could say. Japanese. Long, tangled-up name. Starts with Kumi, so I call him that."

"Does he live in, Mr. Akins?"

"Well, yes and no. Tenth floor, it's mostly servants'

rooms. Go with the apartments. The room numbers match the apartment numbers. Kumi stays in one of those. One that goes with this apartment."

"He'd be there now?"

"I doubt it. Doubt if he'd be back. He's usually off on Thursday, but he wanted to make it today. Didn't ask him why. One day's as good as another, far's I'm concerned. What's the point of all this, Lieutenant? Thought you were interested in Sue Perkins, not my domestic arrangements."

"Sorry," Shapiro said. "Guess I got sidetracked. I do sometimes." He was aware that Tony Cook was looking at him. He did not look at Tony Cook. "Mrs. Perkins called you," he said. "Seemed upset, you thought. Go ahead, Mr. Akins. She wanted to see you, I take it?"

"Something she wanted to take up with me, was the way she put it. Something she wanted to talk about here, instead of waiting until I got in to the office. Didn't make sense. She—well, I thought she sounded gaga, if you know what I mean. Never knew her to be like that in all the years she's worked for me. All right, it worried me. We've—well, we've worked together for a lot of years, you see. Grown sort of fond of the old girl. So I told her to come on up. That I'd wait for her. Frankly, well, I was afraid she was going to quit her job. As if things at the office weren't already bad enough, what with Frank—"

He let it hang there. Sylvia Bradley walked away from the glass side of the big room and sat in a chair a little nearer to the three men. She did not say anything. She merely looked at them. It was rather as if she had just entered the room.

"Was that actually why she wanted to see you, Mr. Akins?" Shapiro asked. "To resign her job?"

"Nothing like that. Nothing at all like that. The damnedest thing. Listen to this, Syl. She wanted me to take that husband of hers in as a partner. Make him creative executive. Take over Frank's job. She kept saying, 'It's only right. It's the only fair thing.' She kept saying things like that over and over. And crying. Half the time she wasn't even coherent. It was—it was a hell of a thing, Lieutenant. She—well, she seemed just to have fallen apart. Jesus!"

"What did you tell her, Mr. Akins? Not, I suppose, that you'd do what she wanted?"

"Hell, no. Mostly I told her to try to calm down. Maybe, that I couldn't decide a thing like that without talking to Mrs. Bradley. Letting her down easy, I suppose you'd call it. She was almost hysterical, I'm afraid. Kept saying we owed him that. After what we'd 'done to him,' was the way she put it."

"Speaking of her husband," Shapiro said. "What did she mean by that?"

"Oh, he used to work at the agency. Copywriter. Did for years, actually. He and Sue met at the office. After Frank joined me, we had to let him go."

"Was that your idea or Mr. Bradley's, Mr. Akins? You say Mr. Perkins had been working for the agency for years. Before Mr. Bradley joined it?"

"Oh, all right. It was Frank's idea. Perkins always seemed like a good man to me. But—well, you don't quarrel with a new partner about a minor matter of personnel, you know. Anyway, from what I hear, Perkins is doing all right. Free-lancing, I understand. So, why Sue'd got all steamed up about it, I don't know."

"You yourself were satisfied with Mr. Perkins's work, Mr. Akins? It was Mr. Bradley who—"

"Frank couldn't stand the sight of him," Sylvia Bradley said. "It was like Frank. He had phobias, I suppose you'd say. If we're not going out to dinner, Leslie, I'd like another sherry."

Akins got a chilled bottle out of a cooler at one end of the room. It was Tio Pepe, Tony noted. He hoped Rachel's scrambled eggs had turned out all right and that she was getting the rest she needed. He hated the thought of her being bushed.

Akins poured chilled sherry into Sylvia Bradley's glass. He looked reflectively at his own empty glass. Then he carried his cocktail glass and the Tio Pepe bottle back to the bar. He put the bottle in the refrigerator and took another bottle out of it. He dropped ice cubes into a squat glass and poured from the second bottle. Tony Cook could not see the bottle he poured from, but assumed it was Jack Daniel's. He did not add dry vermouth. He carried the refilled glass back and sat down with it.

He did not offer drinks to Shapiro and Tony Cook. Cook lighted a cigarette.

"Couldn't stand the sight of him, Mrs. Bradley?" Shapiro said.

"Ugly," she said. "Freakish. He couldn't bear to be around that kind. Had a phobia about it. Always baffled me. Never could understand that about him. Some of my best friends are freakish."

Shapiro recognized the paraphrase. He suspected he was supposed to.

"After Mrs. Perkins had made this request of you," Shapiro said. "This, you say, almost hysterical request, what happened, Mr. Akins? She left? Didn't say where she was going?"

"No. Oh, I offered to take her back downtown. To the office. Said we'd talk it over when—well, when she was calmer. And when I'd had a chance to think it over. All right, I was trying to let her down easy. Temporizing, I suppose you'd call it. She just sat on that sofa over there and cried. And moaned. Now and then—well, it was almost screaming. When I talked to her she didn't seem to hear me. I couldn't seem to get through to her at all. Never went through anything like it, Lieutenant. And this was Sue Perkins! Solid as a rock, she'd been for years. Relied on her, I always had. And now that! I couldn't believe it was happening."

He shook his head, underlining his bewilderment.

"Not like her at all," Akins said. "No control at all. It was as if she were in shock of some sort."

Shapiro had met Mrs. Sue Perkins only once, and then briefly. She had seemed like a very controlled woman. And a very decisive one. There are times, of course, when even the most decisive, the most poised, lose control.

He watched Leslie Akins shake a bewildered head once more and lift his glass and drink from it. For some seconds, then, he held the glass in front of him and looked at it, as if, in it, he might read an explanation of the inexplicable. When he finally put the glass down on the table, it was with a perceptible clink.

He looked at Nathan Shapiro then. He said, "It was the damnedest thing, Lieutenant. Hard to believe it really happened. And I had an appointment at eleven with a client. New client at that. Might turn out to be an important account."

He shook his head again.

"I can see that it made a difficult situation," Shapiro said. "How did you get out of it, Mr. Akins? Since, you say, she wouldn't listen to you?"

"Just sat there crying and shaking her head," Akins said. "No condition to go anywhere, seemed to me. Do anything."

"So?"

"I made some coffee for her," Akins said. "Thought maybe it would help her pull herself together. Instant coffee. Kumi has a gadget I don't know how to work. Brought her a cup and asked her if she wanted cream and sugar. Trying to act as if nothing had happened, you know. Said, 'Just drink this, Sue.' Trying to get through to her."

"Did you?"

"I guess so. Sort of, anyway. She did drink the coffee —with cream, as I remember. And I said I had this client coming to the office at eleven and that she knew that. She'd set it up, of course. And that it was important. Then I said something like, Why didn't she just stay here until she was feeling better? Just stay here and rest. And make herself some more coffee, if she wanted it. That she knew where the kitchen was."

"She did? Know where the kitchen is, I mean?"

"Oh, yes. She'd come up here a few times in the evening. To finish up work we hadn't had time to at the office. Three or four times that happened, at a guess. Once or twice she made us both coffee when we'd finished. Before I phoned down for a cab and sent her home."

"Yes," Shapiro said. "This morning she agreed to stay here until she felt more up to things?"

"Yes. Oh, she still didn't say much of anything. Maybe, 'All right.' And nodded her head. She was still sobbing. Sort of—gulping, if you know what I mean. I hated to leave her like that, but what more could I do? Come to that, I thought she might quiet down better alone, if you see what I mean, Lieutenant."

Shapiro said he saw. And that, then, Akins had left Mrs. Perkins finishing her coffee and gone down to the office? And about what time had that been?

It had been ten or a little after. "You got to my

office about the same time I did, Lieutenant. I had a quick look at my mail and then talked to you. Took up most of the time before my appointment, way I remember it."

"And when you came back here this evening, Mrs. Perkins had gone, I take it?"

"Of course. I don't suppose she stayed here long. Must have steadied down, I'd think. Anyway, she washed her cup and put the cream pitcher back in the refrigerator. So I guess she was all right."

"Probably she was," Shapiro said. "And you've no idea where she might have gone from here, Mr. Akins?"

"None whatever. Not to the office, I know. And you say she didn't go home."

"No," Shapiro said. "She didn't go home, Mr. Akins. We're sorry to have kept you both from dinner."

11

THEY WALKED DOWN the flight of stairs to the twenty-first floor and waited for the elevator to respond to its summons. It did not loiter. Inside, Shapiro pressed a button and the doors closed, and Tony said, "Do we believe him, Nate?"

"Oh," Shapiro said, "I think Mrs. Perkins was there. Probably for the reason Akins says—to get her husband a job. Bradley's death does leave a gap, apparently. One that will have to be filled."

"A convenient gap for the Perkinses," Tony said. "And she could have got into Bradley's office without anybody's noticing."

"Yes," Nathan said. "There's that, of course, Tony."

The elevator had been plunging down at an uncomfortable speed. Much sooner than Tony expected, it stopped. The stopping was as peremptory as the descent had been. A light came on behind the numeral 10. The doors opened. Somebody had signaled the car to stop, Tony assumed. But there was nobody waiting in the corridor.

Tony said, "Hell," and reached toward the bank of buttons. But Nathan Shapiro said, "What we want, Tony," and Tony followed him out into the corridor. "A detective is always curious," Nathan told him.

The corridor was reasonably wide and stretched in both directions from the elevators. There were doors regularly spaced on either side of it, and the doors had numbers on them. On one side, the numbers were even, on the other side, odd: 8A-X, 8B-X, if they went to the right; 7B-X, 7A-X if to the left.

"Match the apartment numbers, apparently," Shapiro said. "Four apartments to the floor, evidently. Must charge like hell for them, wouldn't you say? But maybe it's co-op, not rental. Penthouses ought to be on the up side, wouldn't you say?"

They went to their right. They went the length of the corridor. At its end, they came to a door marked "PH-A-X." X for what? Tony wondered. The unknown? Or, conceivably, xenophobia?

Shapiro tried the knob. Expectedly, it did not turn. Kumi would not leave his door unlocked. He tried the bell push. The ringing sounded loud beyond the door. Nothing else happened and Nathan rang again, and again they waited. And then they heard footfalls. They were slow and uncertain; they clicked on a wooden floor. If Kumi was coming toward the door, he was wearing hard heels.

The doorknob began to turn. It moved only a little. Then it stopped. Somebody was fumbling with it, Nathan thought. Somebody whose grasp was uncertain, indecisive. The knob turned again, slowly.

Then the door swung open, swung inward, violently. Sue Perkins, clutching the inner knob, was falling with the door. Shapiro was quick enough to catch her before she hit the floor. She was limp in his arms. Together, they got her into a fairly large corner room. There were windows on two sides of the room, and the blinds were drawn on both of them. In the inner wall, a bathroom door stood open. There was a daybed, neatly made up, but with the impress of a body on it. They laid Sue Perkins on the bed.

"It can't be morning yet," Sue Perkins said, and she seemed to be speaking from far away. "Can't you let me sleep, Lee? I'm so—" She did not finish. Her voice merely faded out.

"There's a doctor's office downstairs," Shapiro said. But Tony Cook was already looking for a telephone. He found it and dialed "Desk." He got, "Desk. Can I help you?"

"There's a doctor's office in the building," Tony said. "We need him up here. This is police business."

"Dr. Holcombe's office hours end at four," the desk clerk said. "I don't—you said *police business?*"

Tony had. And he wanted to be put through to Dr. Holcombe, if that was possible. If it was not, he wanted Dr. Holcombe's telephone number. He got, "We-ell—"

"Now," Tony said.

"I don't—"

"*Now*," Tony said. "Snap out of it, man."

"We're not supposed—" the man said. "And you seem to be calling from one of the servants' rooms, sir. But—all right, if it's police business. I'll try the doctor." Then there was the signal sound of a telephone ringing. After three rings, there was, "Dr. Holcombe's residence."

The doctor was at dinner.

Tony was Detective Anthony Cook of the New

York Police Department. He was in room PH-A-X on the tenth floor. It was an emergency.

"The doctor doesn't like—well, I'll see."

There was a considerable pause. Then there was, "This is Dr. Holcombe. What's this Stella's trying to tell me?"

Tony told him what it was.

"All right," Holcombe said. "Sounds like too many sleeping pills to me, but I'll be up. Actually, I'm an eye man. Ought to have a G.P., you know. If you can find one. But, all right, I'll come up and have a look at her."

Sue Perkins appeared to be sleeping peacefully, if rather heavily. Asleep, her face had softened. She looked younger asleep.

"Try to get her to drink some coffee?" Tony said.

Shapiro said they'd better wait for the doctor, but that it wouldn't do any harm to have some ready. Or to look around a little. Tony found a hot plate and a sink and a refrigerator behind a screen in a corner of the room. There was also a cupboard. Everything was miniature in size and very neat, except for a tall glass on top of the refrigerator which had, Tony thought, contained milk. It had not been washed. Tony didn't touch the glass. He found instant coffee in the cupboard and a small teakettle. He put water on to boil.

There wasn't much looking around to do in Kumi's room. There was a container of milk in the refrigerator and part of a stick of butter and half a loaf of bread. Kumi evidently did his cooking, for himself and his employer in the penthouse.

The bathroom was immaculate. There was a fresh bath towel on a rack. Tony opened the mirror door of the medicine cabinet, using a piece of toilet tissue. Toothpaste, a bottle of Maalox, a small bottle of an advertised laxative. And a smaller bottle with some bright yellow-and-white capsules in it. The bottle had no label and was about three-quarters full. He left it where it was.

Nathan Shapiro had pulled a chair up beside the daybed and was sitting on it, looking at Sue Perkins, who showed no signs of waking up. Nathan was looking very thoughtfully at the sleeping woman. His face was, as usual, entirely despondent. Tony told him he had put on the water for coffee and what he had found in Kumi's bathroom.

"Nembutal, by the looks of it," Tony said. "No label. These days, the way they slide the label down inside the bottle, anyone could slide it right back out again."

He told Nathan of the unwashed glass. Nathan said, "Mmmm," with no comment in the sound. Then the doorbell rang.

Oliver Holcombe, M.D.—Shapiro suddenly remembered what had been lettered on the plaque on the ground floor, outside the building entrance—was of medium height and probably in his fifties. He had a squarish, pleasant face, which was deeply tanned. He wore a subtly checked sport jacket which, Tony thought, probably had cost him plenty and carried a black bag. He said, "Well, gentlemen, what have we here? One of you called me?"

Shapiro told him who they were. He pointed toward Sue Perkins, who had stirred just perceptibly at the sound of the opening door. "We're hoping you can tell us, Doctor," Shapiro said.

Dr. Holcombe took a stethoscope out of his bag and listened to Sue Perkins. He opened her mouth and used a tongue depressant to look down her throat. When he took the depressant out, Sue Perkins said, "Don't do that, Leon. Don't *do* that." Then she tried to turn over on her side, but Holcombe restrained her. She said, "*Please,* darling," and went back to sleep.

Holcombe took a small instrument out of his bag. He lifted her right eyelid, and, from the device he held, threw a sharp, narrow beam of light into the eye. He looked through the other end of the device he held, and moved the beam around in the eye. He said "Mmmm" and examined the other eye. He said "Mmmm" again and stood up.

"Seem to be in excellent condition," he said. "Seldom seen healthier eyes, as a matter of fact."

"Otherwise?" Shapiro said.

"Other—? Oh, she's asleep, Lieutenant. Just asleep. Rather deeply, of course. Nothing to worry about, that I can see. Probably wake up good as new in a few hours. No actual symptoms of a serious overdose. Just needs to sleep them off. I'm an ophthalmologist. But I don't think any qualified man would tell you different. Of course, you can get her into a hospital, if you're worried. Or just try to wake her up enough to get some strong coffee into her."

"Sleep *them* off, doctor?"

"Yes, of course. One of the barbiturates, I'd think. Oh, possibly chloral hydrate. Somebody likely to have been giving her knockout drops, Lieutenant?"

Shapiro said he didn't know. Tony said, "Nembutal, doctor?"

"That would do it," Holcombe said. "A couple of hundreds—hundred-milligram capsules, that is—or maybe three or four. Or twice as many fifties, of course. Depends on how long ago she took them. And how susceptible she is. Beginning to come out of it, as you've both noticed. She live here? Work for somebody here? Somebody in one of the penthouses, I'd gather?"

"Not as a domestic," Shapiro said. "No, she doesn't

live here, Doctor. A man named Kumi lives here. Yes, he works for a man who lives in one of the penthouses. We'll try to get her to drink some coffee. Sorry to have had to break in on your dinner. If there's a bill?"

"No bill," Holcombe said. "When she wakes up, tell her she doesn't need to worry about her eyes. Won't have to for years, probably." He started for the door. He stopped and turned back. He said, "You going to arrest her for something, Lieutenant?"

Shapiro said, "Thank you for coming up, Doctor." Holcombe looked amused. He nodded his head. He went out and closed the door behind him.

"Are we, Nate?" Tony said.

"Not at the moment, I shouldn't think," Shapiro said. "Not until we wake her up, anyway. Make the coffee strong, Tony."

Tony made it strong, two rounded teaspoons to the cup. He held her up. Nathan said, "Mrs. Perkins!" He said her name several times, each time more loudly than the time before. After his third try, she opened her eyes and said, "You don't have to yell at me." She looked at him through eyes no longer completely clouded by sleep. She said, "Who are you? What do you want? Why are you—" Then her voice trailed away again, and her eyes closed. Tony shook her gently.

"We want you to wake up, Mrs. Perkins," Nathan said. "We want you to drink some coffee and wake up."

She opened her eyes. Shapiro held the cup to her lips. She turned her head away.

"Too hot," she said. "And you put something in it, didn't you?"

Nathan told her that it was just coffee, and that it was better hot.

"That's what you said before," she said. "No, it was too cold then, wasn't it? Who are you? Do I know you?"

"Lieutenant Shapiro, Mrs. Perkins. And Detective Cook is holding you. We talked to you yesterday. At the agency."

"You're the ones who made her sick. Made Amelia throw up. I know who you are. You're policemen. Oh—oh, of course."

"Yes, Mrs. Perkins. Try to drink your coffee now. It will make you feel better."

For a moment, she merely looked at him. Her eyes were rounded. There was doubt in them, Shapiro thought—question in them and suspicion in them. But sleep had almost gone out of them. Abruptly, she took the cup out of his hand and drank from it. She drank all of it. He took the empty cup from her and she started to cough. After a few seconds she controlled the coughing.

"Sunday throat," she said. "Down my Sunday throat. Am I in jail? I didn't do anything to be in jail."

Nathan held the empty cup toward Tony Cook. Cook put pillows behind Sue Perkins and let her relax against them. Her eyes stayed open. He took the cup and carried it to the miniature kitchen.

"No, Mrs. Perkins," Shapiro said. "You're not in jail. As soon as you're up to it, we're going to take you home."

"I just asked him," she said. "Asked him to be fair about it. That's all I did."

"Yes, Mrs. Perkins, I know," Nathan said. He was always saying he knew when he didn't. "Your husband's worried about you. You should have told him you weren't going home from the office."

"He'll understand," she said. "He always does. He'll—" But then she closed her eyes again. Tony came back with another cup of coffee. This time she drank it more slowly. It did not go down her "Sunday throat."

And her eyes opened again. After a third cup of very strong coffee, she swung her legs off the daybed and stood up. For a moment, she swayed a little. Tony steadied her. Then she walked, almost firmly, to the bathroom and into it. She closed the door behind her. Tony raised his eyebrows.

"She'll be all right, I think," Shapiro said. "Coffee's a diuretic. May as well set it up with the lab boys, Tony."

Tony used the telephone to set it up with the lab boys. Routine must be adhered to. Somebody had handled the glass which had, probably, contained milk. And dissolved Nembutal, perhaps emptying the powder out of the capsules? Somebody had touched other surfaces, probably including the door of the medicine cabinet.

He had finished his call to the lab boys when Sue Perkins came out of the bathroom. She looked more fully awake. Probably splashed cold water on her face, Nathan thought. He turned at the sound of a key in a lock.

A small Japanese started to come into the room and stopped abruptly. He wore a rather tightly fitting dark suit and an expression of complete surprise. There was nothing inscrutable about this Oriental face.

"It's all right, Kumi," Shapiro said. "You are Kumi, I take it? We're not burglars. Police officers."

Kumi bowed, a little irresolutely. He said, "Gentlemen." He said, "Good evening, Mrs. Perkins." The surprise was still on his face—and curiosity.

She said, "Good evening, Kumi."

Kumi was looking at Shapiro.

"You've been out all day, Kumi?" Shapiro said. "Or have you stopped back—for a glass of milk, for instance?"

"Yes—no, sir. That is, I have been out all day. Not stopped back. For anything."

Tony, at a slight nod from Shapiro, asked Kumi to step into the bathroom with him. He opened the cabinet door with another piece of tissue and pointed to the little bottle of capsules. "Yours, Kumi?"

Kumi stared. "You found that in here?" Tony waited. "Sir, I never saw it before."

"Do you, by any chance, know what those capsules are?"

Kumi said, "I—no, sir."

"O.K." Tony motioned Kumi out of the bathroom. He said, "We'll be leaving now with Mrs. Perkins, but some other policemen will be along soon. They shouldn't take long. Meantime, don't touch anything. All right?"

Sue Perkins was saying, "Lieutenant Shapiro?"

"Yes," Shapiro said. "Whenever you're ready. Oh— I want to make a telephone call first."

He dialed a number he had memorized. He was answered immediately. There was eagerness, there was anxiety in the answering voice.

"Shapiro," Nathan said. "We've found your wife, Mr. Perkins. She's perfectly all right. Just got—tied up. We're bringing her home."

"I knew she would be," Perkins said. "Kept telling you that, didn't I? Said all along there was nothing to worry about."

The worry—the worry which was really fear—had gone out of his voice. Shapiro said, "Yes, Mr. Perkins, you told us that." (And tried to make yourself believe that, he thought.) "We'll be right along with Mrs. Perkins."

She walked steadily enough to the elevator. They walked on either side of her, just to be sure. On the rather long walk across the lobby she, once, staggered a little, and Tony took her arm. She shook his hand away.

Her decisiveness was beginning to come back, Nathan thought. She walked steadily enough to the parked police car. There was a parking ticket under one of the wipers.

"Some damn fool!" Tony said.

"Nothing to show it's a police car," Nathan told him, and put the ticket in his pocket. It was not one of his major worries.

They had an easy run downtown to the Perkinses' apartment. From the quickness of his response, Shapiro thought, Leon Perkins had been waiting with his hand on the doorknob. The fat man, who did not look grotesque anymore to Nathan Shapiro, held out both hands to his wife, and she said, " 'M all right, dear."

"Of course you are," Perkins said. His voice shook a little on the words. "Of course you are," he said again, and his voice was steady.

"She's fine, Mr. Perkins," Shapiro said, and then, "We'd like to see you in the morning, Mrs. Perkins. Talk things over a little. Shall we come here?"

"I'll be at the office in the morning," she said. "Mr. Akins will be counting on me." The resolute words were, nevertheless, slightly run together.

Perkins put a plump arm around his wife as he closed them into the apartment.

In the car, Shapiro called precinct on the radio. Well, if it was all that important, they'd have a man keep an eye on the Perkins place. They were short-handed as it was. The lieutenant ought to know that. But, O.K.

"House arrest?" Tony asked, and started the motor.

"We could call it that, I suppose," Nathan said. "Or protective custody would be another way of putting it."

Tony pulled the car away from the curb. He said, "You have dinner before you came over, Nate? Because

173

I could do with some food. Maybe we should grab a sandwich?"

"We were just getting ready to eat," Nathan said. "Rose was just about to put the fish on. She'll have eaten by now. Probably put the fish in the freezer. And made herself a salad. Been married to a cop for quite a while now. Getting used to it, I suppose."

"You hope," Tony said. "I had to walk out on Rachel. Know of a decent hamburger joint around here?"

Shapiro didn't. It wasn't the right part of town. And, at almost nine o'clock, it wasn't the right hour, either.

"This Ad Lib place where Akins and Bradley had lunch yesterday," Nathan said. "Ought to be around here somewhere. From what you say, it's open evenings."

The restaurant called Ad Lib still was open. There were people at the bar. Only about half the tables in the restaurant were occupied. Ricardo still had a sheaf of menus under his arm.

Ricardo said, "Good evening, Mr. Cook," the hesitation before the name barely perceptible. It is part of a headwaiter's task to associate faces with names. No, of course it was not too late for them to have dinner. If they would step this way, please?

The table for two was at the wall on their left as they went into the restaurant section of Ad Lib. Yes, they would have drinks, a sherry—"Not too dry," Shapiro said, with resignation in his voice—and a dry manhattan. They looked at the menus. Shapiro said, "Ouch," in a soft, sad voice when he looked at the right-hand column.

Tony said, "Yeah."

The waiter who brought their drinks was tall and

blond. He said, "Would you care to order, gentlemen?" and then looked fixedly at Tony Cook.

"Yes, André," Tony said. "It's me again. And this is Lieutenant Shapiro. He's police, too. But this time we've just come for dinner."

André said, "Gentlemen."

They ordered, with deference to the right-hand column.

Nathan's sherry was not as dry, which was to say sour, as he had feared it would be. Tony wondered why he had ordered a dry manhattan instead of Jack Daniel's on the rocks and decided an association had got stuck in his mind. He looked around the restaurant and remarked, in a low voice, that he'd be damned.

"Probably," Nathan said. "Why at the moment, Tony? Something wrong with your drink? There doesn't seem to be a cherry in it."

"Cherry?" Tony said. "Why, for God's sake, a—oh. Cherries don't go in dry manhattans, Nate. Twist of lemon. No, the drink's all right." He leaned across the table closer to Shapiro. He spoke in a very low voice.

"Corner table," Tony said. "Behind you. Other side of the room."

Nathan turned in his chair, trying to make the movement appear without intention, thinking he was not being at all good at that.

He need not have bothered. Sylvia Bradley and Leslie Akins, at a table in the far corner, were not looking at him. They were looking at each other across the table. Akins, with a cocktail glass lifted partway toward his lips, was listening to Sylvia Bradley, who was leaning a little toward him and talking intently and, from the movement of her lips, rather rapidly. And Akins, with his back to Shapiro, was slowly shaking his head. Mrs.

Bradley could have seen Shapiro looking at them. Apparently she didn't. She saw only Leslie Akins, who seemed not to be agreeing with what she was saying.

Nathan watched them for only a few seconds before he turned back to Tony Cook.

"Well," he said, "they did say they were going out to dinner. Came quite a way downtown for it, I agree. A favorite place of his, apparently."

"They'll think we're following them," Tony said.

"Perhaps," Nathan said. "If they notice we're here. And being pretty obvious about it, they'll think." He sipped from his glass. "Sue Perkins could have done it, Tony. Gone into Bradley's office before she went to the washroom. Lavatory, rest room—whatever they call it. Done her pushing for the afternoon. Got back in time to answer Akins's summons."

"Eliminate Bradley so her husband could get his job back," Tony said. "Get a better job, she hoped. She did go to Akins to make her pitch. It figures, Nate."

"If we believe Akins," Shapiro said. "But Perkins doesn't want the job back. Doing all right as is." He sipped again from his glass. It wasn't as sweet as he liked, but it was better than some. "If, of course, we believe Mr. Perkins," he added. "They still there, Tony? Don't look too hard."

Tony took a quick glance, not moving his head, keeping it casual.

"Just being served," he said. "Both having lobsters. She's putting a lobster bib on. They're having champagne with them. At least, he's brought the bucket. Celebrating, apparently."

"Could be just the way they live," Nathan said. "The way the other half lives. The other tenth of one percent's more like it. Fifteen percent of millions, apparently. Less office expenses, of course. Plenty to support a champagne habit, at a guess. And, no Bradley to split down the middle with, is there? If that's the way they did split it."

"Not precisely a wake, is it, Nate? What they seem to be having? If we believe Perkins, you say. Who do we believe?"

"Everybody," Nathan said. "Nobody. Like always. We—"

He stopped, because Tony Cook did not seem to be listening. Tony was looking across the room. He was making no pretense that he was not looking. When he spoke, it was out of the side of his mouth, his eyes still on the table across the room.

"She's standing up," Tony said. "Taken the bib off. Now she's dropped it—more or less thrown it—on the table. Almost thrown it at him, way it looked. She looks —well, she looks mad as hell about something."

Shapiro turned in his chair.

Sylvia Bradley was standing in front of her chair. She did look upset; perhaps, as Tony had said, the expression on her face was one of anger. She was also talking. People at a nearby table were looking at her. Nathan could not see that Akins was answering what, from their distance, appeared to be a tirade. Akins was merely shaking his head.

Akins stood up and pulled the table toward him. She went out from behind it and walked, rapidly, to and down the shallow steps to the barroom. She did not look back. Akins stood and watched her. When she had gone beyond the bar and out of the restaurant, he remained standing for a moment. Then he sat down again and began to eat lobster. He seemed, from the distance, expert at eating lobster.

"Lovers' quarrel, Nate?" Tony said.

"Could be, Tony. They are, at a guess."

"Or were?"

"Or were. Or it may be merely a disagreement between business associates, I suppose. She was rather, well, standoffish at the apartment, didn't you think, Tony? As if they'd been rubbing one another the wrong way before we got there?"

Tony Cook nodded his head. Then he said, "Look, Nate. If they were that way, playing games together, it— well, it's another angle, isn't it?"

"Oh," Nathan said, "it has been all along, Tony. With Bradley spending his winter vacations in Jamaica, or wherever. And his wife maybe going on cruises. Or, of course, maybe not going on cruises."

André brought them food. No, they did not want wine with their steaks.

"By the way, André," Shapiro said. "Mr. Akins comes here for lunch, quite often, I understand. Happen to know whether he was in today?"

"I did not serve him, sir," André said. "His usual table is on my station, but I did not wait on him today. He may have had something to eat in the bar, sir. Some of our customers do, sometimes. If they are in a hurry."

Shapiro said, "Thank you, André," and cut into his steak. It cut like a good steak should, he thought. Tony looked at him for a moment, and then he, too, began to eat.

When they went out of Ad Lib, it was around ten-thirty. Ricardo was no longer waiting in the bar section to welcome customers. Larry was still behind the bar, but he was sitting down.

They had been very busy that day at lunchtime, he told them. Not that they weren't always busy. How was he to remember who had been in? Even among their regulars. Yes, he supposed he had mixed the usual number of dry manhattans. He didn't remember he had mixed one "the way Mr. Akins likes them." Yeah, some of the regulars had the waiters identify that way, by name. Sometimes Mr. Akins specified that way, and sometimes he didn't. He was pretty sure Mr. Akins hadn't had a drink at the bar, but, no, he wasn't entirely sure. Could be Martin had served him. Yeah, Martin helped out when there were a lot of customers all at the same time. Yeah, they sometimes served food at the bar tables. Sandwiches, mostly. No, he didn't serve food at the tables. Henri did that. Henri was the bar waiter.

"Could be," Nathan said, "Mr. Akins didn't have time for lunch. Could be, he had other things to do."

12

Rose Shapiro was in her bed. She was reading in bed— reading Jane Austen. There was a clipboard beside her on the bed. She had been making notes on paper clipped to the board. Doctorates, Nathan was beginning to realize, are not easily come by. He took off his jacket and his gun before he sat on the edge of Rose's bed.

"I froze the fish," Rose said. "Did you remember to eat, dear?"

"Heartily," Nathan said. "In a rather flossy place. Not, unfortunately, on the city. You?"

"A shrimp salad, dear. Yes, darling, shellfish. And don't go out and look at that picture of your father, will you?"

Nathan said he wouldn't. Then he answered the question her eyebrows asked. The answer was, "No. It's still the mess it was. And it's still possible he took that

Richard Cory's way. Which the defense will argue, if we ever get a defendant."

"But you can't leave it there," Rose said.

"No, darling, we can't leave it there," Nathan said, and took off one of his shoes. "If you wanted me to be made—oh, an inspector, would you push somebody out a window?"

"A current inspector? To create a vacancy? I shouldn't think so, Nathan. Would depend a little on the current inspector, I suppose. But you don't want to be an inspector, do you? You don't even much want to be a lieutenant. There isn't a lot about this one in the papers. Usually, I'm more or less able to keep up."

"Bradley was an advertising executive," Nathan said. "Partner in an agency. Newspapers don't like to annoy advertising agencies. Don't look in their closets for skeletons." He took off the other shoe and sat looking down at it. Rose could not see his face, but she knew it was a very sad face—an entirely dispirited face.

She said, "You'd better go to bed and go to sleep, dear. You've had a long day."

Nathan turned and looked at her.

"No," Rose said. "You look—well, worn out."

"Most of the day, we've been looking for a witness who wasn't there," Nathan said. "When we finally found her, she was three-fourths asleep."

"Frustrating," Rose said. "Go to bed, darling."

Nathan kissed his wife—and took the clipboard off her bed—and went to his own. He did not go to sleep quickly. It was not that the thing didn't have a shape. The trouble was that it had too many shapes. It still had too many when he went to sleep. He couldn't see where Mr. and Mrs. Brook, and a TV script about them, came into it. His last awake thought was that perhaps they didn't. Then, briefly, he dreamed he was falling out a window. But Rose caught him before he hit bottom.

* * * * *

Rachel would be asleep. She wouldn't appreciate being waked up any more than she had this morning. On the other hand, perhaps she might. Tony wrestled with alternatives for a time. Then better—or was it worse?—judgment prevailed, and he went home and to bed. His alarm was set for a quarter of seven. He reset it to ring at eight. That would give him plenty of time to join Nate at the offices of Folsom, Akins & Bradley at nine-thirty.

Tony Cook dreamed, briefly, that Rachel's face was on the side of her head, but awoke enough to remember that was the way one of the crazy painters she posed for had drawn her, and not at all the way she was. Some painters see the damnedest things.

* * * * *

At nine-thirty, Mrs. Perkins was not yet in her office. The receptionist rang to find out. Well, yes, she supposed it would be all right if they waited for her in her office. No, Miss Kline didn't appear to be in yet either. Mr. Akins and Mr. Brad—oh—Mr. Akins usually didn't get in until around ten. His personal secretary was always in her office when he arrived. They knew the way?

They knew the way and took it. There was nobody in Sue Perkins's office. Cook opened the door from her office into the large corner office of Leslie Akins. There was nobody in that office, either. The door to the adjoining office, which had been Frank Bradley's, was closed. There were only two chairs in the Perkins office, and one of them was behind her desk. Shapiro sat on what could, presumably, be called the guest chair. Tony Cook leaned against the wall.

"Did you dream up a revelation overnight?" Shapiro asked.

Tony had not. He noted that revelations were not his department. Of course, Mrs. Perkins could have gone into Bradley's office instead of to the washroom, when Amelia Kline heard her footfalls in the corridor. And it was remarkable what women sometimes would do for their men—even men who looked like Leon Perkins.

"Yes," Shapiro said. "And probably he doesn't look the way to her he does to us. To any outsider."

"Maybe," Tony said. "Perhaps to her—"

He stopped because they could both hear the click of approaching heels on the corridor tiles.

Sue Perkins came into the room. She was wearing a high-collared black dress today. One of the "little black dresses" Rose sometimes mentioned her lack of, Nathan thought.

Sue Perkins did not look sleepy this morning. She looked alert—and decisive.

"I'm sorry I'm a little late," she said, with no sorrow evident in her voice. She sat on the chair behind her desk. She said, "I'm fine, thank you," in response to Nathan's inquiry. "About yesterday—"

"Before we go back to yesterday," Shapiro said, "perhaps you can help us out a little on one or two things about the agency. It's strange territory to us, you see. Oh, there are people in the department who do know about such things, of course. The department has a lot of experts. But Cook here and I aren't among them."

Sue Perkins wasn't quite sure what he was getting

at. Nathan was not particularly surprised. Of course, she wanted to help in any way she could. Nathan Shapiro was sure she did.

"The way I understand it," he said. "Agencies like this one prepare the advertisements—text, photographs, or, I suppose, drawings—and show them to the people who want to advertise."

"The clients," she said. "Yes, Lieutenant."

"And select the magazines or newspapers, I suppose, in which the ads are to appear?"

"Yes. Although nowadays, most of the approved renderings are for television. Oh, some spots on radio, of course. There aren't as many magazines now as there used to be, you know. Or newspapers, for that matter."

Shapiro said he saw. The words still had a stale taste on his tongue.

"And then," he said, "the client buys the space, or the air time, and pays the agency its percentage. Fifteen percent, I understand."

"It comes to that, yes. It isn't done precisely that way. We, the agency, buy the space or the time sector and pay for the package, if it's, say, a TV commercial. We get billed for the total, less fifteen percent. And pay it. Then we bill the client for a hundred percent and he pays us. Or at any rate, he'd better."

"Doesn't he always? Isn't it pretty automatic, Mrs. Perkins?"

"Of course it is. Oh, once in maybe a thousand times, there's a slipup. Few years ago, there was a big account went bankrupt before it paid. Not one of ours, thank heaven. A fairly small agency, and it couldn't take it. Went bankrupt too. But it almost never happens."

"There must be a lot of money involved," Shapiro said.

"Millions," she said. "And millions."

"What we call the free-enterprise system," Shapiro said. "And Folsom, Akins and Bradley gets its share, I imagine?"

"We're one of the biggest in the association," she said. "The Advertising Agency Association, that is. Yes, we get our share."

"Can you give me any idea what that share may come to, Mrs. Perkins? Over a year, say?"

She shook her head. "I just work here," she said. "If you want figures, you'll have to ask the treasurer. Or Mr. Akins himself. But I don't think they'd tell you. Why do you want to know, Lieutenant? I can't see what it has to do with what you're—working on. With poor Mr. Bradley's fall."

"Nothing, probably," Nathan said. "Just trying to get the whole picture. A very profitable operation, I take it. Profitable partnership for Mr. Akins and the late Mr. Bradley. Have you any idea how profitable, Mrs. Perkins? A split of the profits, I suppose. Fifty-fifty?"

"I believe that was the agreement when Mr. Bradley came in. He brought several accounts with him."

"Including Mini-Motors?"

"Majestic Motors Corporation it was then. Mini-Motors Division of Majestic Motors it is now. Since they started to go in for small cars. Yes, they were Mr. Bradley's clients when he joined the firm."

"You were here when that happened?"

"Oh, yes. It sometimes feels as if I've been here all my life. Half of it, anyway."

Shapiro smiled at her and nodded. He said he sometimes felt the same way about being on the police force. He got no response to this except the continuation of a steady gaze. A wary gaze? Any answer would be only a guess.

"Yours is a very responsible position, I'd suppose," he said. "Secretary to one of the partners in an operation this size. I hope they pay you well, Mrs. Perkins." He didn't, quite, put question into his inflection.

"Do you?" she said. There was frost in her voice. "I suppose you want to know how much, although I don't know why. Or what business it is of yours."

He smiled at her again. He said, "None, I suppose. Just curiosity. Just, as I said, trying to get the feel of an operation like this."

She almost smiled back at him.

"Oh, it's not really all that much of a secret," she said. Some of the frost had gone out of her voice. "If you really want to know, sixteen thousand a year. As of the first of the year. They do pay rather well. Leon was getting twenty-seven five before that stink—before Mr. Bradley had him fired. Yes, mine is a responsible job, Lieutenant. A lot more to it than taking letters. And making appointments. And seeing Mr. Akins doesn't forget them, of course."

She looked at the door to Akins's office. Then she looked at the watch on her wrist. She said, "He's late this morning."

Shapiro looked at his own watch. It was ten minutes after ten. "Perhaps he's already there," he said.

"No. I don't think so. When he comes in, he always buzzes me. Just one quick buzz. To let me know he's there. When he's ready for me to come in—that's after he's gone over his mail—he usually uses the intercom. But he might just buzz again."

"You don't go over his mail first? Sort it out?"

"No. He doesn't want that. One of the mail clerks

puts it on his desk. Unopened, of course. He likes to slit the envelopes open himself, with that dagger thing he has."

There was now a tolerant note in her voice. She was making allowance for the oddities of the male animal and its preoccupation with gadgets. Again, Shapiro smiled and nodded. Smiles seemed to thaw. Again, she almost smiled back.

"About your duties," Nathan said. "Just curious, you know. I'm afraid I don't know just what a private secretary does, Mrs. Perkins. We don't run to them on the force. Not where I stand on the force, anyway."

Except—where you stand—for me, Tony Cook thought. He didn't say anything. He just continued to lean against the wall and listen. One of the things he heard was the closing of a door, he thought the door in the next office—Amelia Kline's office. Then he heard another door close, on his other side. The one at the end of the corridor to Leslie Akins's office?

"Well, you see, actually I'm an executive secretary, which involves—it isn't easy to describe, but—oh, being acquainted with situations that come up with the accounts, and handling—well, to some extent—some of Mr. Akins's contacts. For instance, it might be up to me to screen out people I know he doesn't want to see without offending them—or be more or less cordial depending on whether the person who calls is a seller or a buyer—an actual or potential client, that is. And I write certain types of letters for him to sign—I'm so familiar by now with his phrasing. Or he might dictate the key paragraph of a letter and leave it to me to write the rest.

"Of course, I do all sorts of personal things for him too—especially since he was divorced—that was around five years ago. Ordering shirts for him from Brooks

Brothers. Sending presents—wines, mostly—to clients at Christmas. Things like that. And, of course, making out his checks for him to sign—first-of-the-month checks."

"Electric bills. Telephone bills. Bills from—oh, Brooks Brothers? And his liquor store," Shapiro said. "I see what you mean. Drawn on his personal account, they would be. Checks for the rent of his apartment. For—his car insurance. Life insurance, probably."

"Well, all sorts of things. Not rental on his apartment, as it happens. He owns the apartment. Monthly maintenance payments, yes. And he doesn't own a car anymore. Says they're more trouble than they're worth in town. He has a charge account with one of the limousine rental companies, but mostly he uses taxis. So, of course, no insurance premiums on a car. But that's the general idea. I write out the checks on his personal account and he signs them and I mail them."

"Life insurance premiums?"

"Oh, no. The treasurer takes care of those. That's a company matter, you see. Part of the partnership agreement. Insured in favor of each other, he and Mr. Bradley." She stopped for a second. Then she said, "*Oh.*"

"Quite, Mrs. Perkins," Shapiro said. "A very common custom, I understand. For sizable amounts, these policies, I'd imagine?"

"You aren't fair," she said. "You—you tricked me, didn't you? Now you'll think Mr. Akins—"

"No, Mrs. Perkins. As I said, it's probably a very common practice. How much are the policies, Mrs. Perkins?"

"I won't—"

"Oh," Shapiro said, "we can find out easily enough. Simpler if you tell me. More—well, say it will be more private this way. Less of a nuisance to everybody. But if you won't, you won't."

For a moment she was silent. Then she said, "Two hundred and fifty thousand dollars, Lieutenant. The policies themselves are in the treasurer's safe."

A buzzer on her desk sounded then. The time was ten-twenty. Akins had been late. Now he was letting her know he had arrived. He would, she had said, summon her on the intercom, or buzz again, after he had gone over his mail.

"Now about yesterday," Shapiro said. "Way we understand it, you—"

He stopped, because Sue Perkins had stopped listening to him. She got up from behind her desk and, moving quickly, walked to the door to Akins's office. She opened it without knocking. She said, "Yes, Mr. Akins," in a morning voice, and went into his office and closed the door behind her.

"I thought she waited until—" Tony said.

"Yes, Tony. What she just told us. Wants to warn him, I imagine. Prepare him for policemen. One of the duties of a private secretary. Tell him cops are waiting."

"The girl at the desk outside. The receptionist. Wouldn't she have told him?"

"I'd think so, Tony. But maybe she just stands up and salutes. And maybe, of course, Mrs. Perkins wants— well, instructions. We'll find out, won't we?"

They did not find out for a good five minutes. They had time for cigarettes. They used a tray on Mrs. Perkins's desk to stub them out when they heard the sound of the doorknob.

Sue Perkins came into the room. Leslie Akins, tall and erect—a rather large man on the whole—was immediately behind her. He was wearing a black necktie this morning, possibly as a symbol of mourning for a departed partner. He was wearing a dark summer suit which fitted him perfectly. He said, "Good morning, gentlemen. Is there something more Sue and I can do for you?"

"A few odds and ends, we think," Shapiro told him. "Mrs. Perkins was just about to tell us about yesterday when you buzzed for her. Perhaps you can help fill us in about it, Mr. Akins?"

He looked around the small office, as if in search of another chair.

"I told you all there is to tell," Akins said.

"Yesterday evening," Shapiro agreed. "Just when you and Mrs. Bradley were about to go out to dinner. You did get out to dinner, I hope?"

"You know," Akins said. "Following us, Lieutenant? Tailing us, I believe it's called."

"Keeping under surveillance," Shapiro said. "No, Mr. Akins. Pure coincidence. Detective Cook and I just happened to go there for dinner. Being in that part of town anyway. Now, Mrs. Perkins—but why don't you both sit down? It may take us a few minutes to get things straight."

He got up from the guest chair. But Akins shook his head. He said, "Where?" which was a reasonable enough question. He said, "May as well use my office, I suppose. Have I got anything on for—oh, the next half hour, Sue?"

"Mr. Birnham at eleven-thirty," she said. "You arranged it Monday morning, Mr. Akins."

Akins looked at his watch. "Gives us more than an hour," he said. "Be more time than we'll need, won't it, Lieutenant? Can't be much to add to what I told you yesterday. Come on in."

They went into the big, cool office. Akins went to the tall-backed chair behind his desk; Sue Perkins to a chair, suitably lower-backed, at an end of the desk. There were envelopes unopened, on the desk, and two telephones and an empty ashtray. A letter opener, which did look like a dagger, was beside Akins's morning mail. Shapiro and Cook sat in low-backed chairs—client chairs?—and faced Leslie Akins, so erect behind his desk.

Shapiro felt, vaguely, that he should straighten up, come to attention. The feeling was only a flicker, and it passed like one.

"All right, Mrs. Perkins," Shapiro said. "You telephoned Mr. Akins at his apartment yesterday morning. As soon as you got in, I take it. Said you wanted to see him before he came in to the office. Is that the way it was?"

"Yes, it was that way."

"Did you tell him what it was you wanted to see him about? And why it couldn't wait until he came in?"

"No, I don't think so. I was—well, I was sort of upset yesterday morning. There was something I wanted to ask Mr. Akins. And I was upset and impatient and—well, I didn't want to wait. Anyway, I thought it would be better if we talked about it at his apartment instead of here at the office. More—oh, I don't know. More convenient."

"More private, perhaps? Not so much chance of being interrupted?"

"I suppose so. It could have been that, I guess. Can't you understand? I told you I was upset."

"This is all quite needless," Akins said. His voice was very firm. "I—well, I could guess what she wanted to talk to me about. I told her to come on up. That I'd wait until she got there. She did come up. What more do you want, Lieutenant?"

"For Mrs. Perkins to tell us about it the way she remembers it," Shapiro said. "What did you want to talk to Mr. Akins about, Mrs. Perkins?"

"I told—" Akins said, but Shapiro said, "Please, Mr. Akins," in a tone quite unlike any he had used before. From the expression on his face, the different tone surprised Leslie Akins. He shrugged his shoulders slightly and did not finish his sentence. (He sure as hell had a good tailor, Tony thought. Even the shrug did not disturb the shoulder fit of his jacket.)

"About what, Mrs. Perkins?" Nathan Shapiro said.

She looked at Akins for a moment. She got no prompting from his face, if that was what she was looking for.

"It wasn't fair," she said. "It never was fair. Mr. Akins never thought it was fair. It was just that—it was just Mr. Bradley. All the time it was just him. Just him and that damn persnickety attitude of his. That holier-than-anybody attitude. That's all it was." She stopped and looked intently at Shapiro. "You ought to know about that kind of crazy prejudice, Lieutenant Shapiro. You and your people. I'd think you—" She stopped with that.

"Yes," Shapiro said. "We know about bigotry, Mrs. Perkins. Not precisely the same kind, perhaps, but yes. Was Mr. Bradley anti-Semitic, Mrs. Perkins? Is that what you're getting at?"

"I wasn't getting at anything. I just—oh, was hoping you'd understand. Trying to hope you'd understand."

"Frank wasn't like that," Akins said. "At least not so it showed. He was just—well, I suppose you'd have to say, ultrafastidious about the way people looked."

They were certainly wandering from the subject, Nathan thought; at least from the subject he wanted them on.

"I take it," he said, "that you wanted to see Mr. Akins yesterday about your husband, Mrs. Perkins. About his being re-employed here. Is that right?"

"With Mr. Bradley not here anymore," she said. "And the firm needing somebody to do what he'd been doing. More or less what Leon had been doing before Mr. Bradley moved in, wasn't it, Mr. Akins?"

"More or less, in a way," Akins said.

"Without the title," Sue Perkins said. "Without, God knows, the hundred thousand a year Mr. Bradley was drawing. Isn't that true, Mr. Akins?"

"Frank Bradley was a partner," Akins said. "He brought clients with him when he came in. The cases were of course entirely different, Lieutenant. Sue exaggerates, I'm afraid. I don't mean to say Perkins wasn't a very competent advertising man."

"And still is," Sue Perkins said. She was very decisive again now.

"And still is, I'm sure," Akins said. It had the sound of a polite footnote.

"In short," Shapiro said, "you wanted Mr. Akins to give your husband Bradley's job. Was that what it came to, Mrs. Perkins?"

"Not a partnership," she said. "Of course not a partnership."

"But the job? Make him what you call the creative executive?"

"He's very good. Better than Bradley ever was." She looked at Akins. There was no comment in Akins's expression that Nathan Shapiro could see.

"You asked Mr. Akins to give your husband this

193

job," Nathan said. "By the way, does your husband want it? From what he told me, he's quite satisfied with things as they are. Doing well the way things are."

"Of course he wants it," Sue said. From her tone, Nathan thought Leon Perkins had better want it. "And of course he's doing fine as a free lance."

"Yes, I'm sure he is," Nathan said. "You put this up to Mr. Akins. With what result?"

Akins and Sue Perkins answered that together. Akins was a second or two ahead of her.

"I told Mrs. Perkins I'd consider it," Akins said. "And then—I told you this, Lieutenant—she, well, she more or less blew up."

"He wouldn't say yes or no," Sue said. "He just—oh, wobbled back and forth about it. Said he'd have to think it over. Talk it over with his new partner. That sort of thing. Weaseled around it, was what it came to, didn't it, Mr. Akins?"

"I said it was too soon to make a final decision, was all," Akins said. "I may have said I'd have to talk it over with Mrs. Bradley. She inherits her husband's interest in the agency. I told Mrs. Perkins that. But I'm not sure she listened to me. As she admits, she was upset. You do admit that, Sue?"

"I don't know it's something I *admit*. All right, I was upset."

"You were damn near hysterical," Akins said. "I had no idea why. Haven't now. You weren't rational about it, Sue. Seemed to think—oh, that it was a crisis. Something that had to be decided that very moment. I kept trying to calm you down. You remember that, don't you?"

"I remember double-talk. Your trying to palm me off."

They were beginning to ruffle each other, Nathan thought. Two people at the same time wasn't the way he liked things. A jangling way for things to be. But, since it has arisen, a situation to be made the most of.

"Why were you so upset, Mrs. Perkins?" Shapiro asked. "Because of Mr. Bradley's death? Although I gather that didn't cause you any special grief. And why was there all this urgency about Mr. Akins's decision? All this pressure on him to make up his mind?"

"It was all—oh, all at once things seemed to be coming apart. I don't know. Do people always know why they're upset? I just felt I had to get things settled. Right away. That's how I felt yesterday morning. All—well, torn to pieces. A lot of things, I suppose. Are you a psychologist or something, Lieutenant Shapiro?"

"No, just a cop, Mrs. Perkins. Sometimes cops have to try to find out what makes people tick. But go on about yesterday. You couldn't get a firm decision from Mr. Akins. Then?"

For a moment, she looked fixedly at Nathan Shapiro. Then she looked at Akins. Akins merely raised his eyebrows.

"All right, I suppose I did sort of break up," she said. "It was just so—so frustrating. Like a dream you can't wake up from, however hard you try. I think I started crying and couldn't stop."

"You certainly did, Sue," Akins said. "You—well, you weren't yourself at all. I didn't know what to do with you."

"You brought me something to drink," she said. "Coffee, wasn't it? Something hot, anyway."

"Instant coffee," Akins said. "I thought maybe it would help you pull yourself together. I suppose a tranquilizer would have been more to the point, but I didn't have any."

"Coffee," she said. "A cup of coffee. And you did say something about pulling myself together. I do remember that."

"You drank the coffee, Mrs. Perkins?" Shapiro asked.

Akins answered for her. "She certainly did," he said. "And it did seem to calm her down."

"Way you remember it, Mrs. Perkins?"

"I guess so. Yes, he did bring me coffee and I suppose I drank it. I'm pretty sure I remember that. It was afterwards things began to get muzzy."

"Muzzy, Mrs. Perkins?"

"Sort of—oh, vague. Unreal. As if, right in his apartment, and early in the morning, I was falling asleep. And coffee is supposed to keep people awake, isn't it?"

"Yes," Shapiro said. "Or people think it does, anyway. And then you—"

"She did seem to be falling asleep," Akins said. "I told you about that, Lieutenant. That I told her I had to get along to the office to keep this appointment she knew about and that I wanted her to stay right there in the apartment until she felt more herself. I told you all that. Don't you remember, Shapiro?"

"Yes," Nathan said, "I remember what you told us."

"Hard to tell," Akins said. "The way you keep going over things."

"A habit policemen fall into," Shapiro said. "Often pretty annoying, I suppose."

"To suspects, Lieutenant? Is that what you mean?"

"To anybody who may have information we need," Shapiro said. "Or may need. Sometimes points we'd like slip people's minds, Mr. Akins. The first time around, I

196

mean. And come back later. Often happens, I find. Trivial points, usually. By the way, did you have lunch at Ad Lib yesterday? Or, perhaps, go up to your apartment to see how Mrs. Perkins was making out?"

"I had lunch uptown," Akins said. "Business lunch. All right, with our attorneys. One of the firm, that is. Frank's death—well, it leaves a few points to be straightened out. You'll understand that, Lieutenant?"

Shapiro said he could understand it would.

13

AGAIN, SUE PERKINS was looking fixedly at her employer. And again, Shapiro could see no response in Leslie Akins's expression. He seemed to be listening to something Nathan Shapiro couldn't hear. Or for something. He was not looking at Sue Perkins. He was looking toward the door which, now, closed off the office that had been Frank Bradley's. Movement behind that door? Shapiro couldn't hear any. Amelia Kline had said that the doors to the offices of the two principals of the firm were heavy doors, blocking off sound.

"By the way, Mr. Akins," Shapiro said, "has Miss Kline come in yet, do you know?"

"Yes," Akins said. "Came in the same time I did. Caught up with her just inside, actually. She doesn't look well, Lieutenant. Pretty fond of old Frank, I think she was. Shocked by what happened. As we all are, of course. Are you quite sure he didn't just fall? Lose his balance and fall out that damned window?"

"We're still trying to make sure," Shapiro told him. "What this is all about, really. All our prying into things. If he did, he tried to save himself, you see. Clutched at the windowsill and couldn't hold onto it. Metal sill, you know. Be slippery, particularly if his hands were damp. With perspiration, say. Grabbed the sill with his right hand. The lab men found his fingerprints there. Just a smudge where his left hand would have been. Left hand slipped first, apparently. And then—well, he just let go. Hung on for a second or so and—fell. Probably screamed and nobody heard him. They usually do scream, Mr. Akins. All the way down, usually. Even when they've jumped intentionally."

Akins closed his eyes. He moved his head, slowly, from side to side.

"When they know it's final," Shapiro said. "Know it can't be reversed. Must be a bad few seconds, mustn't it? A few seconds of terror. Like, I suppose, when they tighten the last strap in the electric chair and step back away from you."

Akins opened his eyes and looked at Nathan Shapiro.

"You make it very vivid, Lieutenant. But we don't use the chair anymore. From the way you talk, I gather you've been instrumental in sending people to the chair."

"Juries do that," Shapiro said. "And judges. Used to, as you say. They didn't have to attend, of course. Yes, we're not quite so barbaric nowadays. In this state, anyway. But this isn't getting us anywhere, is it? And you say you have an appointment, Mr. Akins. With Mr. Birnham, I think you said."

Akins nodded his head. He also looked at the watch on his wrist. Shapiro turned to Sue Perkins. She was still looking at Akins. It was, Shapiro thought, as if she were waiting for him to do something. Or say something.

"Mrs. Perkins," Shapiro said, and she started a little. But Shapiro had not raised his voice when he spoke her name. Her eyes left Akins's face reluctantly, it seemed.

"Yes?" she said, after a second.

"You got drowsy in Mr. Akins's apartment yesterday morning," he said. "Did you actually go to sleep? Or just feel, as you put it, muzzy?"

"I must have gone to sleep," she said. "A bell waked me up—partly waked me up. I thought it was the telephone and then realized it was a doorbell and that I had to go to the door. And the door was—way off. Miles away, it seemed like. And then I—no, that's not right, is it? Because you and the other detective were there. But that can't be right, can it? Because I wasn't in the apartment, was I?" She paused for a moment and Nathan thought there was bewilderment in her eyes. "It still isn't clear, somehow," she said. "It's all mixed up in my mind. Confused."

"No," Shapiro said, "you weren't in the apartment when we found you. Don't you remember where you were, Mrs. Perkins?"

"Almost. Wasn't it in Kumi's apartment downstairs? Wait. Kumi—he's Mr. Akins's servant, you know —came in after you waked me up, didn't he?"

"Yes. And that's how you knew where you were? Knew you were in Kumi's room?"

"Yes. I suppose so."

"And you hadn't know before?"

She shook her head.

"But you knew where his room was? On the tenth floor with the other rooms for servants."

"Vaguely," she said. "That one floor of the building was for servants' rooms. For living-in people. You must have told me that, Mr. Akins. One of the times you had me go up to the apartment to finish up some work. Didn't you?"

"I may have," Akins said. "I don't remember. Anyway, apparently you found it."

"Obviously she did since we found her in it," Shapiro said. "Do you remember going down to the tenth floor in the elevator, Mrs. Perkins? Finding the right room? Unlocking the door and going into Kumi's room?"

"No. Wait a minute. How would I unlock his door? Where would I get the key?"

"What I was wondering," Shapiro said. "Unless Mr. Akins gave you one when he left you in the apartment to, as he says, have time to pull yourself together. Did you, Mr. Akins? You have a key to the room, I suppose?"

"Certainly. After all, the room goes with the apartment and I own the apartment. It's—oh, it's around somewhere, I suppose. No, I didn't give it to Sue here. Why should I?"

"I don't know," Shapiro said. "Kumi was off all day yesterday, Mr. Akins?"

"After he'd fixed my breakfast. I told you he wanted off, although it wasn't his regular day. Thursdays and Sundays are his regular days. He's usually here Tuesday afternoons to—oh, sort of keep tabs on the cleaning crew—two women, I think it is—they come in and go over the place. Move everything around, damn it. In spite of Kumi. Nothing's where it ought to be Tuesday evening."

"I know," Nathan said. "We have a cleaning woman come in once a week. Nice enough girl, but she always pushes the books back as far as they'll go on the shelves. Rose—Rose is my wife, Mr. Akins—keeps telling her not to, but every Wednesday Rose has to pull the books out again. Wednesday's the day our cleaning woman comes, you see."

(Tony Cook realizes that Nate Shapiro sometimes moves in what appear to be circles. Often, he can tell what Nate is circling toward. This time he couldn't.)

"Thought you might possibly have given Mrs. Perkins the key so she could go down to Kumi's room so this cleaning crew wouldn't disturb her," Shapiro said. "If it took her several hours to—get herself pulled together. But you say you didn't."

"No, of course not. I supposed she'd be feeling herself again in—oh, half an hour or so. When did you and Detective Cook find her, Lieutenant?"

"Oh, quite late. After we'd talked to you and Mrs. Bradley. Held you up when you were ready to go out to dinner."

"Then she must have been there all day," Akins said. He turned to Sue Perkins. "I don't understand that," he said to her. "What was it, Sue? Some sort of reaction to your having been so—upset about something? Was that it?"

She looked at him for several seconds without answering. Then she said, "I don't—" But Shapiro cut her off.

"After we found her," he said. "And had a good deal of difficulty waking her up, we got Dr. Holcombe to come up and have a look at her. The doctor who has his apartment on the ground floor of the building your apartment is in, you know."

Akins nodded his head to show he did know. He said, "Eye specialist, I understand. You had him up, you say?"

"Yes. He said she had taken a rather large dose of some sleeping medicine, he thought. Was pretty sure, actually. But that it obviously wasn't a lethal dose. One of the barbiturates, he thought, but that she was coming out of it all right. Do you remember taking sleeping pills, Mrs. Perkins?"

Again, she was slow in answering. She seemed to be thinking of something else. When she did answer, she spoke very slowly. "No," she said. "I never take sleeping medicine. I never have any real trouble going to sleep. I—"

But she did not finish. They waited a moment, but she did not go on.

"Of course," Akins said, "Kumi may just have forgotten to lock his door. When he went off to his movies. He does on his off afternoons, he tells me."

"It's a snap lock," Shapiro said. "Have to adjust it so it wouldn't automatically lock after him when he closed the door."

"Perhaps he was expecting somebody," Akins said. "A friend. And left the door unlocked so he could get in. Or she, I suppose."

"Perhaps," Nathan said. But he was not looking at Akins. He was looking at Sue Perkins, because she looked as if she were about to speak. But instead of speaking, she looked away from all of them and out the window. Shapiro looked where she was looking and couldn't see anything to account for her gaze—except, of course, a considerable area of downtown Manhattan. She did not turn toward him when, finally, she spoke.

"Milk," Sue Perkins said. "Only that was just a dream, wasn't it?"

"I don't know," Nathan said. "You dreamed about milk?"

She turned toward him then.

"It's all mixed up," she said. "The way dreams are. It couldn't have been real because it was wrapped in paper. So it couldn't have been real, could it?"

"The milk was wrapped in paper, Mrs. Perkins?"

"Of course not. That would be silly. The glass the milk was in had paper around it. And somebody said, 'Drink this and you'll feel better.' "

"Did you know who said that?"

"No. Whoever it was was a long way off. Only the hand—the hand that put the glass down, of course—that was quite near. Only the voice was a long way off. You can see it was just a dream, can't you?"

"Where were you when you had this dream, do you know?"

She shook her head.

"Maybe I was at home," she said. "Maybe it was last night I had the dream. Or maybe it wasn't a dream. Maybe last night I waked up and Lee brought me a glass of milk. It's all—all mixed up in my mind. It's just something I dreamed about, Lieutenant. I don't know why I'm boring you with it."

"You're not boring me, Mrs. Perkins," Shapiro said. "In this dream, did you—?"

Akins did not let him finish the question.

"Well," Akins said. "It's boring me. All of this is." He looked at his watch again. "And I told you I had an appointment."

"Yes," Shapiro said. "With Mr. Birnham, wasn't it? The man who wants to build a commercial around this mystery film. I'm afraid Mr. Birnham will have to wait a few minutes. In this dream, Mrs. Perkins, did you drink the milk? Or don't you remember?"

"I don't—no—yes, I do. I remember I was surprised it was so cold. Leon always takes the chill off before he brings it to me, because I don't like it cold."

"You drank the milk in this dream of yours," Shapiro said. "Then what, Mrs. Perkins?"

"I must have gone back to sleep," she said. "Do we

have to go on and on about this silly dream of mine?"

"No, I don't think we do," Nathan Shapiro said. "Yes, Tony? You wanted to ask Mrs. Perkins something?"

Tony hadn't been aware he'd showed it. But it did seem to him there was something Nate had missed. Not that Nate hadn't circled to something interesting.

"When you asked Mr. Akins here to give your husband a job, Mrs. Perkins," Tony said, "did you have some reason to think he'd agree? Out of hand, I mean?"

"Some reason? I don't know what you mean by reason, Mr. Cook. I just hoped he would. Because it would have been the only fair thing to do. Because they hadn't been fair to him before, you see."

Tony looked at Nathan Shapiro. It was a way of passing him the ball.

"What Detective Cook means," Nathan said, "did you feel yesterday morning that you had pressure to bring on Mr. Akins? The kind of pressure that might persuade him to do what you wanted?"

The answer was very quick.

"Of course not," Sue Perkins said. "How could I bring what you call pressure on a man like Mr. Akins? A man I've worked for for years? You make it sound— why, you make it sound like *blackmail*."

Shapiro looked at Leslie Akins. Akins smiled. There seemed to be tolerance in his smile.

"You do rather, Lieutenant," Akins said. "I'm sure you didn't mean it that way, but it did sound a little like it, don't you think?"

Nathan looked at the big, erect man for a few seconds. Then he said, "Perhaps. I see how you might get that idea. Nothing to it, you'll probably say."

"Of course I'll say," Akins told him. His voice was peremptory, harsh. It had been, for the most part, a noticeably relaxed voice until then. "What are you trying—?"

He stopped in the middle of that sentence. They could all hear what stopped him—the faint grating of metal against metal, as a doorknob turned. The door to what had been Bradley's office opened, opened somewhat violently. Sylvia Bradley came into the room, her movement as abrupt as the door's opening.

She had a sheet of paper in her right hand, and she waved it excitedly at Leslie Akins. There was none of the previous evening's detachment in her manner, nor, when she spoke, in her voice.

"So he *did* go through with it," she said. "As he told me he was going to. As you told me he hadn't and never—"

She seemed then for the first time to realize there were other people in the room. She completed her sentence with an *"Oh!"* which was an explanation. It had almost the force of an expletive.

"I didn't know," she said. Then she held the sheet of paper out to Akins. He took it loosely; merely glanced at it. Then his fingers closed as if he were about to crumple it. And then, more sharply than he had spoken before, Shapiro said, *"No,* Mr. Akins." Akins looked at him. "We'll have a look at it," he added and moved to Akins's desk and held his hand out. After a moment's hesitation, Akins gave him the sheet of paper.

It was a carbon copy of a letter, typed on the letterhead of Folsom, Akins & Bradley, and dated the previous Monday. It read:

Leslie Akins
Folsom, Akins & Bradley

Dear Leslie:

In accordance with paragraph 2 of our letter agreement of October 1, 1971, I am withdrawing from our partnership as of today. I take this step with reluctance, and for personal reasons which I am sure you will understand.

As further provided in the agreement, I am reclaiming the option granted me by Timothy Langhorn, author, for television and other performance rights to certain characters created by him in novels titled "Brook No Evil," "Brink of Death," and "The Glass Knife," the characters specified in the option agreement being those of Enid and Paul Brook. Other characters in these three novels are also, as you will recall, listed in the option agreement.

This option, which has not been exercised, was assigned by me to the agency when we entered into partnership, with the stipulation that, if the partnership were dissolved on the initiation of either of us all rights granted in the option would revert to me.

Again with regret that I am forced to make this decision,

Sincerely yours,

The letter, although in carbon, was signed, "Franklin Bradley."

Shapiro looked at the bottom of the sheet. He would have expected to see "FB/ak." He did not.

He folded the carbon of Bradley's letter and started to put it in his pocket.

"I'll take that," Akins said.

Shapiro shook his head and pushed the letter down

into his jacket pocket. "I believe the carbon would belong to the writer of the letter. Or, as in this case, to his estate. Not to the recipient of the original, Mr. Akins. I take it you did receive the original of this one?"

Akins said, "Do you?" which, of course, was no answer at all.

"Tony," Shapiro said, "will you see if Miss Kline is in her office? And if she is, ask her to come in here for a few minutes."

Tony went out through the door which opened directly on the main corridor. While they waited, nobody said anything. Sue Perkins continued to look through one of the big windows at Manhattan's jagged and eventful skyline. Sylvia Towne Bradley sat on one of the numerous chairs in the office and pulled her skirt down over her knees. It was the skirt of a sleek blue-and-gray dress, which complimented a figure Nathan hadn't realized Sylvia Bradley had.

Amelia Kline came into the room ahead of Tony Cook. She looked even smaller than she had looked the day before, and even more drained. Shapiro got up and motioned toward his chair. She sat on it and looked at Leslie Akins, who did not particularly look at her, and waited, small and silent.

Shapiro drew another chair up and sat beside her. He took the carbon of Bradley's letter out of his pocket and said, "I'd like you to look at this, Miss Kline," and gave it to her. She looked at it and then at Nathan Shapiro.

"Did you type it?" he asked her.

She shook her head. "No," she said. "I never saw it before. Mr. Bradley did his own typing every so often. Memos to clients, sometimes. And outlines of ideas he suggested to the writers. Most of his letters he dictated to me, of course. Not this one, though. Only—"

He waited, but she did not go on. He said, "Only, Miss Kline?"

She looked at Akins, who, again, did not look at her. She waited a second. Then she said, "Mr. Bradley gave me an envelope addressed to Mr. Akins and told me to put it on Mr. Akins's desk, where he couldn't fail to see it. The envelope was sealed. Perhaps this letter was in it."

"When was this, Miss Kline?"

"It was—it was Monday. Last Monday. The day Frank was—" Her voice faltered. Then it stopped.

"Yes, Miss Kline," Shapiro said. "What time last Monday?"

"Just before they—Frank and Mr. Akins—went out to lunch. He told me to put it on Mr. Akins's desk after they had gone."

"And you did?"

"On top of some other letters he hadn't opened yet."

"Mr. Akins, you got the letter? And read it. I noticed you didn't bother to read it just now. As if you knew what was in it."

"Yes, I read the letter."

"His decision came as a surprise to you? I mean, he hadn't mentioned dissolving your partnership while the two of you were having lunch?"

Akins hesitated a moment before he said, "No, Lieutenant."

"These personal reasons Mr. Bradley speaks of," Shapiro said. "Which he is sure you will understand. Did you understand them, Mr. Akins? Know what he was talking about?"

"No," Akins said. "I've no idea what he was talking about."

"You, Mrs. Bradley?" Shapiro said, and turned toward her. She seemed to rejoin them; to come back with a start from some distant place. She said, "What?"

"The personal reasons your husband mentioned? Do you know what they were? When he told you he was going to dissolve the partnership, did he tell you why?"

"No. He did say a strange thing, though. He said I'd know why."

"But you didn't?"

"No. I had no idea what he meant. I told him I didn't and he said—well, he said, 'Come off it, Syl.' Not in the way he usually spoke to me. He was usually—well, polite. He always made a point of being."

"Just—polite, Mrs. Bradley?"

"I don't know what you mean by that, Lieutenant Shapiro. Why you use that tone."

"All right," Shapiro said. "When was this, Mrs. Bradley? This conversation with your husband?"

"Monday morning. Quite early Monday morning. He must have called from the apartment. I'd just finished breakfast. I'd been going to go riding."

"You were surprised he was going to quit the agency? He hadn't talked about it with you before?"

"Never. He never talked much about the office. Oh, I thought once or twice that he was a little restless. He had his own agency before he and Leslie joined up, you know. Perhaps he missed—well, being entirely his own boss. Running things his own way, you know. But I never thought it really bothered him."

"And you think that may have been what he meant when he wrote Mr. Akins about personal reasons?"

"I don't know. I can't think of anything else. I really can't, Lieutenant." She was very emphatic. Needlessly emphatic?

"When you came in a few minutes ago—" Shapiro began. He stopped because one of the telephones on

Akins's desk rang. The ringing seemed very loud. Sue Perkins got up from her chair and moved toward the ringing phone, but Akins shook his head and picked the telephone up and said "Akins" into it. They could all hear the sound of a woman's voice, but could not hear the words.

"All right," Akins said. "Tomorrow, then, if he's feeling up to it. If you'll just let Mrs. Perkins know. Oh, tell him I'm sorry. They can be nuisances."

"Birnham's come down with a summer cold," Akins said, as he put the receiver back in its cradle. "Takes care of that for today. Check with them first thing in the morning, will you, Sue?"

Sue Perkins said, "Certainly, Mr. Akins." She continued, however, to gaze out the window.

"When you came in here, Mrs. Bradley," Shapiro said, "you said, 'He *did* do it,' as if you hadn't thought he would. 'Did go through with it,' you said. You hadn't expected him to? And you understood from Mr. Akins that he hadn't?"

"Yes, I suppose so. Maybe Leslie didn't actually say he hadn't. I may just have gathered that from—oh, what he didn't say, if you know what I mean."

"Yes," Shapiro said. "After your husband called you Monday, you didn't go riding, I take it. Came into town, instead. Went to see your lawyers downtown. Your lawyers and the agency's lawyers. Is that right, Mrs. Bradley?"

"Yes, I came in to see Mr. Goldstein. But it was about another matter entirely. Nothing to do with any of this."

"All right," Shapiro said. "This morning, you came into your husband's former office. To—to do what, Mrs. Bradley? To see if you could find what you did find?"

"Frank told me he had already written a letter to

Mr. Akins. Leslie—well, you did tell me last night, Leslie, that you hadn't got any such letter. Didn't you, Leslie?"

Akins looked at her. He raised his eyebrows and shook his head.

"You did, though," she said. "Anyway, I knew if Frank had written the letter, or dictated it to his secretary, there'd be a carbon. He always made carbons of everything. Even of letters to friends. It's the way he was. So—well, I stayed in town last night. At the apartment. And came down here early to look. Just when the office was opening. A lot of the help was coming in. The people who work here, I mean. And I just came in with them. Nobody said anything to me. So I went on to Frank's office. It took me quite a while to find the carbon. But I kept on looking and I found it. And—well, brought it in to show Leslie. I didn't know there'd be other people here."

"Yes," Shapiro said. "Mr. Akins, you admit you read this letter. What—"

"Admit? What do you mean, 'admit'?"

"Don't deny you read it, if you prefer it put that way," Shapiro said. "What did you do with the original after you'd read it? Give it to Mrs. Perkins to file? Or file it yourself? Or—take it in to Mr. Bradley in his office and say—oh, 'Come off it, Frank. You don't really mean this. Why don't we just tear it up?' Something like that."

For seconds, Leslie Akins merely stared at Shapiro. But his fingers crept toward the daggerlike letter opener. Shapiro said, *"Tony!"* and Tony Cook moved quickly. He took the dagger from Akins's desk and carried it back to his chair. He ran a finger crosswise on the blade. He looked at Nathan Shapiro and nodded his head.

"Well, Mr. Akins?" Shapiro said.

"I didn't see Frank after I read his letter," Akins said. His voice was heavy. "I stayed right here at my desk. Mrs. Perkins can tell you that. I was dictating letters to her."

Shapiro looked at Sue Perkins. She wasn't looking out the window anymore. She was looking at her employer. Shapiro said, "Well, Mrs. Perkins?"

"No, Mr. Akins," Sue Perkins said. She spoke very slowly. "No, I can't tell him that. Because you weren't here when I first came in. You came in after a few minutes. Two or three minutes, I'd think. In through that door." She pointed at the door she meant.

Akins's right hand moved on his desk. He seemed, Shapiro thought, to be groping for the knife which wasn't there any longer. Which Tony Cook held, and across the edge of which he was slowly, abstractedly, running two fingers.

But the searching movement of Akins's hand wasn't evidence, of course. Neither was the way he looked at his private secretary.

"I'd like to use your telephone if I may, Mr. Akins," Shapiro said. "Which is the direct line?"

Akins looked at Nathan Shapiro for a second. There was a set expression, which amounted to no expression at all, on his face. Then he pointed to one of the two telephones on his desk. Shapiro went to the desk and spun the dial. He said, "Captain Weigand, please. This is Shapiro."

There was a brief pause. Then, "This is Lieutenant Shapiro, Captain." (The formality would let Bill know there were civilians listening.) "The Bradley case. I'm bringing four witnesses in, captain. Will you send the D.A.'s office a signal, sir?"

Nate was, Tony Cook thought, rather laying it on. Tony stood up. He was still holding Akins's paper knife.

He put it down on the seat of the chair he had vacated. He couldn't see that they'd be needing it.

"Mr. Akins," Shapiro said, "I'm afraid I'll have to ask you to come down to the squad headquarters with us. You too, Mrs. Perkins. And you, Mrs. Bradley, and Miss Kline. There'll be a few more questions, you see. With somebody from the District Attorney's office sitting in."

The women stood up first. Akins remained seated, behind his desk. He said, "Ask, Lieutenant?"

"I'd appreciate it," Nathan said. But he spoke in his policeman's voice.

Akins put both hands flat on his desk. He put weight on his hands as, slowly, he stood up. He seemed to need the help of hands.

14

On Thursday, the eight-to-four ended at a few minutes after four, which was entirely unlike it. Wednesday's eight-to-four had ended after midnight. Since all New York's taxis were someplace other than East Twenty-first Street, or had gone home for the night, Tony Cook had had to walk home through the still steamy night. (He could, of course, have taken the Lexington Avenue subway to Grand Central, shuttled to the Seventh Avenue and gone downtown again to Fourteenth—and then walked the rest of the way. It hadn't seemed worth the trouble. He had been in a fog anyway: had felt that everything was in a fog.)

The fog hadn't cleared much by Thursday afternoon. He did find a cab. An early drink, followed by a shower—tepid—helped some. So did clean clothes, getting into which was interrupted by a brief, and unplanned, nap. He felt pretty much himself as he climbed to the Gay Street apartment. He felt more like himself with each upward step. When he answered Rachel's "Hi" with one of his own, he thought he felt fine.

"You look tired," Rachel said. "You sound worn out, Tony. You should have called and said you weren't up to anything. You—"

He kissed her to stop her talking nonsense. She was wearing a sleeveless light-green dress and his first inclination was to help her take it off. But she freed herself, and he made them drinks. After he had poured Tio Pepe into her chilled glass, he made himself a martini.

"A quick picker-upper," he explained and was told he sounded like a TV commercial.

"But I can't remember for what," she added.

"No product identification, that's your trouble," Tony said, and sat down on the sofa beside her. "Fault of a creative executive somewhere, I shouldn't wonder. God, the way they talk. Advertising people, I mean."

"Yes, dear, I know what you mean. I've been exposed. But it's over now, Tony. Anyway, the *Post* seems to think it is. With this man Akins in jail. And the girls out on bond as material witnesses. Are they pretty girls, dear?"

"I'm glad you asked that," Tony said. "Reveals a proper feeling. Sort of, in different ways. The Kline girl is, anyway. Or will be, when she grows up. Mrs. Bradley looks as if she played a lot of golf, or tennis or something, in the sun. Which, I take it, she does. Mrs. Perkins—well, run-of-the-mill. First-run, yes. No, Rachel, it isn't over. Nobody's happy about it. Weigand isn't and Nate isn't and, for what it's worth, I'm not. And the man from the D.A.'s office said, in effect, 'Yah. All right, you can go ahead with it, but yah.' "

"He doesn't think you've got the right man?"

"No, it's not that. He agrees with Nate. Akins killed his partner because the partner was going to pull out and pull at least three of their biggest accounts with him. Two he'd brought in and one—well, one he'd just picked up. Cut Folsom, Akins and Bradley down to size—to less than half size, probably. This way, Akins keeps the accounts, along with a quarter of a million in insurance, or expected to. He also expected to keep Mrs. Bradley—one way of putting it. Marry her, maybe. Looks that way, anyhow. Only—it seems she started to turn against him when he wouldn't admit her husband had dissolved the partnership. Nate and I saw her walk out on him, you know, Tuesday night at the Ad Lib."

Questioned by Shapiro and Assistant District Attorney Bronson at the headquarters of Homicide South, she had admitted that on Monday morning she had gone to see her lawyers about divorcing Bradley; that when he had told her about pulling out of the agency, he'd also said he wanted a divorce. Said that if she wouldn't get it, he would. Claimed he had grounds. She said of course he didn't have grounds, but she'd been about ready to divorce him anyway—but the next thing she knew, he was dead. And then, when she began to believe that Akins was, for some reason she couldn't fathom, lying to her, she'd—as she put it—"walked the floor all night."

"And the next morning," Tony said, "she tracked down Bradley's carbon in his files. Which is, of course, what precipitated Akins's arrest. Only, the D.A.'s man says, how're we going to prove Akins is a murderer when we can't prove there was a murder?"

"Does seem to be a point there," Rachel said, and sipped from her glass. "Can't you?"

"We can try," Tony said. "Bronson—he's the guy from the D.A.'s Homicide Bureau—thinks we shouldn't have too much trouble with the grand jury, what with the fingerprint on the milk glass from Kumi's room, but

217

a trial jury—well, he doesn't know. Because, how can we prove Bradley didn't fall out that damn window? Three stiff drinks, a light lunch—ladies and gentlemen of the jury, wouldn't that be inclined to make any man woozy? Unsteady on his feet? And Akins has got Williams in his corner. Almost always gets his clients off, Williams does, according to Bronson."

Rachel said, "Mmmm." She said, "Speaking of drinks, Tony dear." Conversation had slowed Tony's consumption. He took care of that. He mixed a fresh martini and poured sherry from the chilled bottle into a glass fresh from the freezer. He sat down again beside her.

"So," he said, "you can see why nobody's very happy about it. Except Akins, maybe. How did things go with you today, dear?"

"I stood on one foot," she said. "Literally, I mean. The way the photographer wanted it. So joyous I was about to take off, I gather. Seems I'd just taken something with iron in it. Made me feel like flying. You'd think it would be the other way around, wouldn't you? Fingerprint on a milk glass, Tony?"

"Milk with sleeping medicine in it," Tony said. "For the benefit of Mrs. Sue Perkins. Akins's fingerprint. Right index. He thought it was all neatly wrapped up in paper toweling but, well, he slipped up. Hard to wrap a glass without touching it. Particularly one full of milk with, say, half a dozen fifty-milligram Nembutals dissolved in it. The pill bottle was wiped clean, by the way. This is—well, not public property, Rachel."

Rachel said she wasn't public and sipped from her glass. Tony said she damned well wasn't and put his glass down on the table. All right, he told her. It was this way:

Also questioned by Shapiro and Bronson, Mrs. Sue

Perkins had recovered her memory. Part of it, anyway. And what she now remembered about Monday afternoon did not jibe with what Akins had said happened. She had not been sitting at an end of Akins's desk, making shorthand symbols, for ten or fifteen minutes before Amelia Kline had come in to tell them what had happened. Yes, she had agreed with her employer's version. But that wasn't the way it really was.

The way it really was was that he had buzzed for her, not called her on the intercom, just as she was leaving her office to go to the washroom. "Which she calls the ladies'." She had been sure Mr. Akins wouldn't mind. "What, dear? I didn't hear you."

"Sorry," Rachel said. "When you've got to go you've got to go, was all. I didn't mean really to say it out loud. Go ahead, Tony. She went to the john. And?"

She had got back to her office after, she thought, about five minutes. "She said, 'I had to wait.' " She had gone directly from her office into Akins's, carrying her notebook.

"And Akins wasn't there. It was two or three minutes before he came in. And, Rachel, he came in from Bradley's office. She didn't think about it particularly at the time. Seems they popped in and out between their offices a good deal. What the connecting door was for. But when Amelia came in to tell them that Frank Bradley was a flattened blob seven floors down—sorry, dear. Nasty way to put it. That he was dead."

He paused and drank from his glass. She sipped from hers and waited.

"Well," he said, "then she did begin to think about it. And when, later on, Akins gave us his version she thought about it a lot."

When Shapiro phoned the next morning to say he had a few more questions and was coming along to ask them, she hadn't yet left her office. She had told the office manager she was going to and arranged for a substitute to sit in. She had been explaining a few things to the girl from the pool when Shapiro called.

"She says that, up to then, she'd just planned to go home and think things over. Decide what she ought to do. But, after Nate called, she thought she had better see Akins 'before I answered any more questions,' was the way she put it. She denies, of course, that she planned to use her version to pressure Akins to give her husband Bradley's job. She says, 'That would have been blackmail. That would have been wrong.'"

"She's been reading transcripts, sounds like," Rachel said. "And Akins told her to come on up, I gather. Why, Tony?"

"Recognized a threat when he heard one, would be my guess. It's Nate's guess, too. And Bronson says, uh-huh, seems likely. So she went on up. She still says she broke up when Akins wouldn't promise to do what she wanted. Still denies she threatened him when he wouldn't. She guesses he must have put something in her coffee, but she says she doesn't know why."

"Why did he, Tony? Since he didn't obviously, give her enough to kill her."

"To buy time, we suppose. People in a bad spot do try to buy time. Think maybe something will turn up. Also, a dead woman in his apartment would have been —well, inconvenient. Particularly when he had a cleaning crew coming in that afternoon. Enough to shut her up for a while. Give him time to work things out."

"Can you prove he gave her sleeping medicine, or whatever it was?"

"No. He washed the coffee cup out pretty thoroughly. And if he had a bottle of barbiturate capsules around, it was probably the one we found in Kumi's bathroom. Kumi has now admitted, incidentally, that he had seen a similar bottle containing similar capsules— *and* with a label made out to Mr. Leslie Akins—in Mr. Akins's medicine cabinet. We can't prove it's the same one, of course. He probably gave her one capsule up in the penthouse—perhaps removing the label there—and more of the same in Kumi's room, next time around. But he wasn't so careful the next time around."

The next time around, Sue Perkins now remembered, although pretty vaguely. She did not remember what time it was, but she was almost certain that Akins had come back. "Who else would it be? It's his apartment." And, very vaguely, she remembered being helped along a corridor and into a room, "somewhere else." She was pretty sure she remembered being brought milk in a glass with paper wrapped around it. Yes, she thought she drank it. "It was cold. Leon always takes the chill off before he gives it to me."

There was barbiturate, identified as Nembutal, in the dregs of milk in the glass that had the print of Akins's right index finger on it, and plenty of Sue Perkins's prints on it. Why he hadn't washed the glass, as he had so carefully washed the cup, and why he hadn't just pocketed the little bottle of capsules, they didn't know.

"Might have been afraid Kumi would show up," Tony said. "Or anyway was in a hell of a hurry to get to the office. To be seen there. Got there about when Nate did, as I remember. Was rattled, maybe, and slipped up. Often they do, luckily. A big help, sometimes. Whether it will be big enough this time—well, I told you why we aren't happy. Why Nate isn't, I mean."

"Won't the fingerprint prove he drugged her,

Tony? To keep her from talking? And talking about what, except his coming in from Bradley's office? She will testify to that, won't she?"

"Says she will. Yes, dear, that's what Akins's lawyer is going to have to explain to twelve men and women. And that's why Bronson gave us the go-ahead on a homicide charge. And Akins can say he did go into Bradley's office and that poor old Frank wasn't there. And that he just supposed Frank had stepped out. And that if the window was wide open he didn't notice it. And that he has no idea how his fingerprint got on the milk glass, unless maybe it was a glass which really belonged in the apartment and that he'd touched it there and that Kumi had taken it down to his room by mistake. Anyway, a lot of jurors don't like fingerprint evidence much. Any more than they like testimony by psychiatrists. And the defense will try to get jurymen as dumb as they come. That's routine, dear."

Tony finished his drink. He said, "The Algonquin? Now that there isn't any Charles?"

"All right, I guess," Rachel said. She finished her sherry and looked reflectively at the empty glass. "And I guess I'm not going to get to be an actress after all," she said. "And after I've learned my part, too. All four lines of it."

Tony Cook had started to stand up. He sat down again.

"I wouldn't give up yet," he said. "Nate's talked to this man Birnham. He thinks, incidentally, that Birnham was originally Birnbaum, or something like that. Says it's any man's choice, of course, if he can get a court to agree. Tolerant about such things, Nate is. Says one man from his father's congregation—man named Isaac Simonsky—wound up as an 'Ian Saxon.' And joined the Unitarian Church. Says Rabbi Shapiro thought it was more funny than anything else. Says the old man says he thought of changing his name to Sherman, but decided against it. That it wasn't approved in the Talmud. I'd like to have known Nate's father, wouldn't you?"

"Yes," Rachel said. "To get back to Mr. Birnham, or whatever. The man Nathan saw today. Who is he, aside from maybe once having been Mr. Birnbaum?"

"Executive vice-president and advertising manager of the Mini-Motors Division of Majestic Motors. A man with millions to spend on advertising. And, dear, a man who had agreed to transfer his account to Bradley, after Bradley left Folsom, Akins and Bradley. A couple of other big accounts had agreed to go along with Bradley too, apparently. A reason to push poor old Frank out the window. There was no prohibition on grabbing clients in the Bradley-Akins agreement, the lawyers say. Usually there is, they told Nate."

"So?"

"So, Sylvia Bradley inherits all of her husband's assets and plans, apparently, to go into the agency business on her own. Hiring Leon Perkins to run the show for her, she thinks. If he wants the job. And our Sue will see that he does, I imagine. And taking Bradley's captive clients with her, of course."

"Yes, Tony," Rachel said, with much patience in her voice, "We were talking about my not getting to be an actress, weren't we? Not that it matters, really."

Tony said he was sorry; that for four days he had been up to his neck in it. "Deeper than that," he said. "Over my head, most of the time."

She smiled at him and took his hand. But when it began to move in hers she said, "No, Tony. The Algonquin. Remember?"

He said, "All right." Then he said, "Among Bradley's assets is this option on Langhorn's characters. The

Mr. and Mrs. Brook thing. Birnham's very sold on a Brook TV series. He's seen Anderson's script and likes it. Says it just needs touching up a little here and there. And is willing to have Anderson direct the pilot. And Anderson likes you in this part."

Rachel said, "Oh." Then she said, "I get killed in the first scene. There doesn't seem to be much future in it, does there? Still—we ought to have another drink or go catch us a taxi."

They caught a taxi on Sixth Avenue. The hacker was from Brooklyn, momentarily trapped in Manhattan. But he agreed that he could go straight up Sixth Avenue to Forty-fourth Street. He had some trouble at Herald Square, but no more than was to be expected. He got them to the Hotel Algonquin. He flicked on his Off Duty sign and took off for Brooklyn.

M

Lockridge
    Or was he pushed?